I0741655

Lord, Help Me to Hold Out!

By

Joy Marino

with

Valerie L. Coleman

Published by

Queen V Publishing
Dayton, Ohio
QueenVPublishing.net

Published by

Queen V Publishing
Dayton, Ohio
QueenVPublishing.net
Info@PenoftheWriter.com

Queen V Publishing is a Christian contract publishing company of standard and integrity. We allow God's Word in you to do what it was sent to do for others.

Library of Congress Control Number: 2009904970

ISBN-13: 978-0-9817436-1-5

Cover design by Candace K
Edited by Valerie L. Coleman of PenoftheWriter.com

Printed in the United States of America

Praise for Lord, Help Me to Hold Out...

"A wonderfully candid look at a woman molded by her life experiences. The book drives home the importance of how early life-lessons influence our development into successful adulthood."

> Michelle Larks, best-selling author of *'Til Debt Do Us Part* MichelleLarks.com

"Author Joy Marino's debut novel, *Lord, Help Me to Hold Out* is a page turner! With an array of believable characters caught up in gripping circumstances, Marino brings to life a novel that entertains, enlightens and uplifts! It is easy for the reader to become engrossed in the book from the beginning to end. Joy Marino will be one to follow as she is sure to quickly climb the literary ladder!"

> Dorinda D. E. Nusum, author of *The Back Pew Crew* DorindaDENusum.com

"A promising new voice whom I suspect will be a mainstay in contemporary literature."

> Dr. Vivi Monroe Congress, best-selling author of *Manna for Mamma*

"*Lord, Help Me to Hold Out* is a voice of hope crying in the wilderness of desperation. Joy's heart for women can be felt throughout the book as she empowers us to know that how a thing begins is not how it has to end."

> Idella McIntyre, Founder of Unstoppable M.E.

Dedication

I dedicate this book in loving memory of three special people:

My grandmother—Beverly A. Leonard-Nash—who taught me the power of trusting God. She convinced me that I was the apple of God's eye. She loved me unconditionally. I miss her so much!

My uncle—Clarence (Sonnie) George, Jr.—who taught me that with hard work and determination all things are possible. I thank him for seeing the vision but most importantly for believing!

My uncle—Rev. Michael George—who helped me press toward the mark and showed me how to truly walk by faith. What a mighty man of God!

Acknowledgements

I want to thank my husband, Carlton David Marino. You have revealed to me the divine revelation that I am esteemed.

Proverbs 18:22

To my beautiful daughters of God, Talia Dior and Basia Rain: It has been pure bliss to watch you relentlessly grow in Christ! Thank you for freely sharing my time with God's ministry. Mommy loves you sooo much!

Proverbs 31:28

To my Mom and Dad: Mom thanks for your wisdom. Dad thanks for your discipline. Thank you both for encouraging me to pursue my dreams.

Proverbs 1:8

To my spiritual mom, Alice Gray: Your divine wisdom, patience, vision and kindness have been a blessing beyond words. You are truly amazing!

Proverbs 31

Special thanks to John Gray, Idella, Theresa, Rashanna, Amber, Proz and Ashton. Your fidelity, time and support were not in vain.

Proverbs 17:17

Chapter One

Hope

A swarm of police, accompanied by the principal, bombarded the classroom. The teacher jumped from her chair and walked to the mob at the door.

"Which student is Hope Jackson," the principal asked.

With her mouth gaped open, the teacher pointed to Hope seated in the middle of the room.

Two of the policemen, girded with guns and handcuffs, walked to Hope's desk. "Hope, My name is Officer Lewis and this is Officer Calumet. We need you to come with us."

Startled, Hope kicked her desk. A pencil rolled to the edge. "What did I do," Hope asked, as tears crawled down her cheeks.

"You didn't do anything," the officer said. He caught the pencil just before it hit the floor and placed it on the desk. "We just need you to come with us."

Hope looked at her teacher, the officer and then back at her teacher.

The teacher said, "It's okay, Hope. Everything will be fine."

Hope bowed her head. She collected her schoolwork,

put on her coat and hat, left without resistance. The other students whispered as the police whisked her away.

Red and blue lights flashed on the six squad cars parked at the school entrance. Puffs of fumes rose from the exhaust pipes. Hope stopped, took a step back. She geared up for an all-out tantrum, but the perceptive principle intercepted.

"Everything will be okay. You didn't do anything." She caressed Hope's hands, looked her in the eyes, said, "These officers are just taking you home to get some clothes."

"But I ---"

"Please go with the officers, honey."

Hope conceded and sat in the back seat of the police car. She stared out the window at the principal and officers who talked for several minutes.

Once off school grounds, the officer in the passenger seat turned to Hope. "You and your brothers and sisters will be staying with your grandparents for a few days."

"Why?"

"Your mother has been in a little accident. She's fine, but she'll be in the hospital a few days."

Hope sat silent.

As the parade of patrol cars rounded the corner to the Jackson home, a host of emergency vehicles awaited. Hope fumbled with the door.

"I have to open the door from the outside." The officer jumped out of the car and opened the back door.

Hope walked down the driveway and gasped. Pools of dark blood oozed from the bright-white snow. Her heart raced as she followed the red trail to the porch.

She peeked inside the front door which was wide open.

The clock with brass spokes that radiated like sunrays was broken and emitting through the screen of the new color television. Remnants of family pictures were shattered on the floor. Wallpaper drooped from the wall. Several uniformed strangers stood in the living room. Hope hesitated to enter.

The escorting officer assured her. "Not to worry, dear. Your mother is fine. We're going to get you a few outfits and then we'll be on our way to see your grandparents." He squatted to look the four-year-old in the eyes. "What special name do you have for your grandmother?"

"Grammy."

"Grammy, that's a nice name." He covered her hand with his and led her through the clutter. She stumbled over a broken table.

"You okay?"

Hope nodded.

They walked toward the bedroom past the bathroom. Pills and medicine were strewn on the floor. Toothpaste spackled the shower door. The busted toilet seat rested in the sink.

Hope crinkled her nose. "What's that smell?"

"It's a special soap we use to clean up."

Every devastated room reeked of the "special soap." A scent that once symbolized cleanliness now represented filth and disgust. As Hope stuffed the broken pieces of her life into a grocery bag, she heard a uniformed stranger say, "So much for a carefree childhood."

Cherries Fall

How can shadows dance and cherries fall while snowflakes turn to blood?

Joy Marino

Blackbirds quickly cloud the sky but all I see are the cherries.

Chapter Two

Sarah

After fighting with irate customers all day, Sarah Jackson spent another hour fighting with perverts and weirdoes on the city bus. Exhausted, she missed her stop and had to walk several blocks to her apartment building. Embarrassed by the click of her worn heels, she tried to walk on the balls of her feet when a passerby came near. She side-stepped past the bag lady who yelled expletives to invisible people, sighed as she began the ascent up four flights of stairs. "I should have finished college."

The hollow apartment door squeaked. Sarah set her purse on the floor, lit a cigarette, took a long drag. She plopped on the couch and watched the ashes drift to the shag carpet.

Hope walked in the front door. "Hi, Mommy." She kissed her mother on the cheek and sat on the floor at her mother's feet.

Sarah gave a gentle tug to Hope's ponytails. "Hey, baby girl. How was your day?"

"Okay. Miss Cathy said that I can't go over there tomorrow."

"Aaagh." Sarah sat up and rubbed her temples. Miss Cathy, her neighbor, had been babysitting for the last few weeks. They had originally agreed to take turns watching each other's kids, but Sarah's long hours far outweighed the few hours Miss Cathy worked. To even the deal, Sarah promised to pay thirty dollars a week. She was three weeks in the red.

Sarah rocked back and forth. "She wants her money and I don't have it." She ran her hands up and down her legs with enough friction to start a fire and then rubbed her temples again. The stress provoked a memory from several months earlier.

The bright sun glistened on the fresh snow of the unseasonably cold Cincinnati winter. Sarah wrapped the scarf around her neck twice and tracked home through eight inches of snow and slush. She needed to change clothes before going to her second job. With her head bowed to thwart the blistering wind and preoccupied with getting to work on time, she didn't notice the car that backed into the driveway or the woman in the passenger seat.

She disrobed to her slip when she entered the house, hurried to the bedroom to get her waitress uniform.

"Jimmy? What are you doing here?" She crossed her arms across her body to cover herself.

Startled, he walked to the window. "Let's see, I've got my suitcase open and I'm taking clothes out of the closet. If I were a betting man, I'd say I'm packing." He pulled back the handmade drapes, looked outside and then continued to pack.

"That's funny." Sarah sucked her teeth, rolled her eyes, grabbed her housedress that hung behind the door. "Speaking of betting, you need to give me some money. It's freezing outside and the utility bill is late."

"I don't need to do anything but get out of here." He

removed the hangers from the clothes on the bed, folded them into the suitcase.

"I don't understand why you're doing this to us." Sarah sat on the bed and rubbed her legs.

"Doing this to you? I'm doing this *for* me." He peeked out the window again.

"What are you looking at?" Sarah walked to the window. Lena, her husband's girlfriend, smirked and waved. "You can't keep bringing your girlfriend around the kids like everything is okay. It's not right, Jimmy. You are still my husband. You promised to love me and take care of me." She swiped at the tears that cascaded down her cheeks. She loved that average-looking man with all of his flaws because he made her feel special. Well, he used to anyway. "You begged me to have these four kids and now you don't want to have anything to do with them. Do you even know their birthdays? Better yet, can you spell their names?"

"Don't get cute with me, Sarah. This marriage was a joke from the beginning. We both knew that I could never be the man your father was, but that didn't stop you from demanding and me from trying." He walked to the dresser, grabbed his underwear. "I hated your nagging and got tired of seeing the disappointment in your face." He stuffed the last of his things in the suitcase and closed it. "Lena doesn't have any expectations of me and I like it that way. She goes with the flow." He walked to the bathroom to retrieve his shaver and toiletries.

Sarah followed close behind. "Well let her flow into paying these gambling debts for you. I'm busting my tail to keep food on the table while you run through women and blow money."

"Just accept that I took you for what I could get. I moved on, why cant you?"

"It's like that? Well since you're all about taking, how about you take this V. D. you gave me and give it back to Lena?"

Infuriated, Jimmy lunged at Sarah. "You won't disrespect the mother of my baby like that."

"Your wha---"

Before she could finish her question, Jimmy threw a right that landed square on her left jaw. The shattered bone splintered and blood ran out of her mouth. She cupped her loose jaw in her left hand and went for the scissors in the medicine cabinet with her right. Jimmy had turned to walk down the hall when the blades punctured his back. He spun around and flung Sarah into the mirror. The glass shattered as she sank to the floor.

Jimmy grabbed the toilet seat which was held in place with one screw, held it above his head. With tight lips and flared nostrils, he said, "I could kill you."

"Well do it then," Sarah mumbled. She spit blood and teeth on his shoes.

"You're not worth it." He smashed the toilet seat in the sink, turned to leave.

Unwilling to give up on her man and her marriage, Sarah jumped on his back. The duo tussled from the bathroom to the living room leaving a trail of destruction like a tornado through Kansas.

Jimmy snatched the sun clock off the wall and threw it at Sarah. A spoke sliced open her right cheek. Blood splattered on the walls. He ran out the front door.

Lena jumped in the driver's seat and revved the engine. Jimmy reached for the door handle and then slipped on the ice. He broke his wrist trying to break the fall.

Weakened by blood loss and holding her face together, Sarah stumbled to the porch. She crawled down the steps. "Jimmy! Why?"

"Open the door, Lena!"

Lena slid to the passenger side and flung open the door. She grabbed Jimmy's coat collar and pulled him into the car.

"Jimmy!" Sarah struggled to stand. She took a few steps, collapsed on the unshoveled sidewalk. "Jim…"

The warm blood that pooled around Sarah's face melted the snow. As she lay in a puddle of crimson and cream, the daylight dimmed.

Sarah massaged her scarred face. "If your no-good daddy hadn't left us for that tramp…"

Twirling her hair, Hope looked up at her mother. "Momma, what's a tramp?"

"A tramp is somebody who tricks your daddy into leaving us." Sarah looked at her oldest child, the spitting image of her ex-husband. "Lena is a tramp, trollop, hussy. Pick a name. Now stop asking me questions and turn on the music."

Hope bit her bottom lip, turned on the Magnavox quadraphonic eight-track tape player. The 1971 hit, *Let's Stay Together* by Al Green filled the space of the two-room apartment.

Sarah stood and swayed to the music as if she had a six-foot slow-drag partner. The tape jammed. "Can I get a break?" Sarah clenched her fists. "Go get your brother and sisters from Miss Cathy. Tell her she'll have her money when I get it."

Hope scurried across the hallway relieved that The Temptations' *Papa was a Rolling Stone* wasn't in the player. For some reason, she endured verbal and physical attacks when that song played.

~~~~~~~~

About a year later, Sarah met and married Mark Tolliver. A kind-hearted man, he legally adopted her four children and blessed her with a fifth. To provide for his growing family, Mark joined the military. He climbed the ranks to officer in the United States Marine Corp, while the family remained in Cincinnati. Once he received his base assignment, he uprooted the family to join him.

Although Mark loved his family and gave all of the children his surname, Hope still missed her father. She had five years of him coming in and out of her life and would spend her life looking for his love.
~~~~~~~~

Chapter Three

David

Despite frequent relocations to military bases across the country, Hope found stability in music and poetry. The calm of lyrical mastery soothed her teenage desires and helped her live up to her parents' expectations of being a good example for her siblings. To stave the lustful passions of youth, she joined the church choir and attended Girl-Scout meetings once a week. However despite her attempts at nerdiness, she found herself drawn to the stereotypical bad boy.

David Hoffman was the coolest high-school boy in Jacksonville, North Carolina. His slow gait gave ample time to preview his flawless mocha complexion and luscious green eyes. With upturned Izod collars, fitted stonewashed jeans and Converse shoes, he smelled like a summer ocean breeze. All of the girls swooned and vied for his attention, but for some reason, he favored a naïve eighth-grader at Beacon Junior High. A bit uncultivated and disreputable, David's gorgeousness did not move Hope's stepfather.

"Hope, I checked around." Mark took off his officer's coat adorned with medals, ribbons and shiny gold buttons. He placed it across the back of the dinette chair and carefully wiped away the wrinkles. Without looking up, he said, "David is in high school."

"Yeah, but he's only two years older than me. You're four years older than Mommy."

Mark clasped his hands together. "He's a troublemaker without a future."

"You told me that you were in your twenties before you knew what you wanted to do with your life. David's just a sophomore." Hope smirked. "What's the big deal?"

"His father is enlisted."

"Are you for real? I can't da--- I mean hang out with David because his dad's not an officer." Hope furrowed her brow and crinkled her nose. "What's that got to do with anything? Mommy hangs out with enlisted women and you work with their husbands. So why can't I date their kid?"

"No dearest, they work *for* me. This is not a democracy, Hope. My mind is made up."

Hope forced a tear and whined. "But Daddy I don't have a lot friends. Every time we move, I have to start all over." She expelled an embellished sigh.

"Baby girl, I know how boys think. I'm not comfortable with you dating yet."

"We're just gonna hang out once in a while. He's not my boyfriend." Hope threw her hands behind her back and crossed her fingers.

~ ~ ~ ~ ~ ~ ~ ~

Although he had a tough exterior, David was a gentle soul. He enjoyed life and shared his dreams of becoming an architect with his girl as they walked hand-in-hand along the marina pier. In these intimate moments, they shared innocent kisses. The relationship was going well and had it not been for the intrusion of others, it may have flourished into more.

Hope bounded down the stairs. Her feathered hair and stick-up bangs—stiff from spray—stayed in formation. "Daddy, David and I are going to the movies. I'll be home about nine." Hope primped in an imaginary mirror.

Sarah wiped her hands on her apron and walked into the dining room. "Wait just a minute, young lady." She inspected Hope's attire and make-up. "Is that glitter on your face?"

"Mommy, everybody wears glitter."

"Well I'm not responsible for everybody." She licked her thumb and attempted to put the spittle on Hope's face.

Hope pulled back. "Ooooo! That's so gross."

Her father chuckled. "Sarah, let that girl be. She looks cute and more important, has everything covered." He hugged his daughter. "What movie are you going to see?"

"I'm not sure. Whatever's playing at the base theater."

"Okay, baby. We'll see you at nine."

As she walked into the kitchen, Sarah called out, "You keep that sweater tied around your waist!"

"Yes Mommy." Hope blew her parents a kiss and danced out the front door.

~ ~ ~ ~ ~ ~ ~ ~

After the movie, David took off his Members Only jacket and put it around Hope's shoulders. Her off-the-shoulder shirt was cute, but not practical for the cool evening breeze.

"Thanks, David."

"You're welcome." He put his arm around her tiny waist and pulled her close. "It's the least I can do for my girl." He leaned in for a kiss.

"Aha!" Mark jumped out from behind the bushes. "Get your hands off my daughter, punk!"

Startled by the ambush, the two jumped away from each other. The jacket fell to the ground.

"Daddy! What are you doing here?"

"Making sure that my daughter's *friend* brings her home the same way she left." He glared at David who stood motionless.

Hope gasped and threw her hand over her mouth. "Daddy, how could you?" Hope looked at David. His beautiful green eyes were wide with fear. She picked up the jacket and handed it to him. "We didn't do anything."

"Only because I stopped him from attacking you. Now let's go."

"But ---"

"But nothing." He pointed to the car. "Homeward bound. Forward march!"

~ ~ ~ ~ ~ ~ ~ ~

Sarah met Hope at the door as she came in from school. The look on her face told Hope that trouble was on the horizon.

"Mommy, what's wrong?" She set her books on the cocktail table.

"I just got off the phone with Patricia." She closed the front door and motioned for Hope to sit on the couch. "She told me that you and David have been skipping school to make out at the marina."

"Mom, that's not true. David and I have never skipped school." The fear of an all-out assault kept David at bay for several weeks, but his heart beat for Hope's affection. He loved the way she played in his mane and twirled her hair when she giggled. They snuck out to the marina on occasion to steal quiet moments.

"Oh, so you have made out?"

"No!"

She looked her daughter square in the eyes. "Hope."

"We haven't. We've kissed a few times, but that's it. I swear!" Hope threw up her right hand as if a bailiff swore her in on The People's Court.

"What do you think kissing is? Tiddly winks? You were making out."

"Mom, no. We barely even touched lips. Making out is what you did with Daddy Jimmy under the bleachers."

Sarah drew her hand back, but decided not to follow through. "Patricia's not the only one telling me about your dates." She emphasized 'dates' by gesturing quotation marks. "Several of my friends have been looking out for you and they all gave me similar feedback."

"You mean those busybodies who have nothing better to do than watch soaps all day and gossip about two teenagers in love." She threw her hand over her mouth.

"Love, huh? Let me tell you about love." For the first time, Sarah told Hope about the abuse she endured from Hope's biological father, Jimmy Jackson. She even shared the gory details of the beating that landed her in the hospital and the kids at Grammy's for several weeks.

Hope cried without restraint. "I had no idea."

"That's because I tried my best to keep that from you. I know how much you love your father."

"I'm sorry that Daddy Jimmy hurt you like that, but why tell me this now?"

"I don't want you to make the same mistakes I did. I fell in love with a bad boy, gave him all of me long before marriage and then watched my life fall apart. We were too young." She paused. "Too young to know ourselves let alone deal with life. That's why Mark and I are so strict about you dating David or any other guy."

"I promise we'll be different."

"Oh, I know you will. We've already talked to his parents."

Hope reared her shoulders back and huffed, "You what?"

"Be careful, young lady. You know I will snatch you up."

Hope bowed her head in retreat.

"They assured us that they would talk with David to put an end to this relationship. I hate to intervene, but that's my job. Believe me; you have your whole life to find love."

Hope grabbed her books and walked toward her room. She mumbled under her breath, "I already found it."

~ ~ ~ ~ ~ ~ ~ ~

The next day, David called Hope.

"You know I really like you, but all this drama is too much for me."

"I like you, too. I'm sorry my folks keep getting in our business."

"We've been good about keeping it clean, but we still get accused of things we've never done."

"We'll have to be more creative with our dates so those nosey folks don't know what's going on."

After a sufficient pause, David said, "Hope, we can't see each other any more."

"Huh? You're not going to let them keep us apart, I know."

"It's just not worth it. My folks came down hard on me."

"You mean I'm not worth it." Hope whimpered, hung up the phone. Daddy Jimmy walked out on her and now David.

Soon after the break up, Mark received orders and the family relocated to Beaufort, South Carolina. Grateful that she had somehow beat the odds of being classified as a total loser, Hope looked forward to the new start.

~ ~ ~ ~ ~ ~ ~ ~

Large plantation-style homes, gas street lamps and oversized shade trees made the historic seaside town of Beaufort seem like a step back in time. Even the horse-drawn carriages moved at a slow, agonizing prance.

Hope took advantage of the small-town pace and forged ahead like a steam engine on steroids. She advanced to an academic honors program and maintained straight As. The frequent moves finally paid off as her knowledge excelled above her new peers. Not only had Hope slipped out of geek mode, she took over the reigns of Miss Popularity. She made captain of the junior varsity cheerleading squad and had an entourage of friends and followers. Smart, cute and athletic, the attention went to her head. She developed an ego the size of the Empire State Building. Life was good!

One day at lunch, Hope and several of her fans had a carefree conversation.

"Hey, Hope. Heard you aced another exam," a red-haired girl with braces said.

"Yeah, you know how I do it." Hope pouted her lips like Betty Boop. The group laughed.

One of the cheerleaders who sported her boyfriend's

letterman jacket said, "You heard about the new high-school guy?"

In synchronized fashion, the group said, "No. Do tell."

"I heard he's absolutely dreamy. Handsome and athletic with eyes to die for." She released an enamored sigh. "He plays on the varsity football team with my boyfriend and will probably make team captain." She flaunted the ornaments adorning the too-big jacket.

"Wow, he must be really good," Hope said, as she thought, It doesn't take much to excel on this island.

"His number is 87," the boyfriend-having cheerleader said. "We've got to go to the game tonight and check him out."

"What do you care? You have a guy."

"Doesn't mean I can't enjoy the scenery."

The group laughed and agreed to sit together at the stadium.

~ ~ ~ ~ ~ ~ ~ ~

The Beaufort Eagles geared up for the game while the marching band played the school fight song. Hope and the crew sat near the section designated for the varsity cheerleaders.

The announcer bellowed through the sound system. "Good evening, ladies and gentlemen. And welcome to the annual rival game between the Beaufort Eagles." He drug out the name and paused for the fans to clap. "And the Goose Creek Gators."

Hope laughed. "What kind of name is Goose Creek?" She and the crew compared outfits while the announcer introduced the starting players.

"Ooo, that get up is too cute and I just love your hair," Hope said to Red Braces.

"And the new Eagles' team captain…"

"Thanks. Took me two hours to tease it up. What are you doing after the game?"

"Number 87…"

"Not sure yet. Wha---"

"Shh," the boyfriend-having cheerleader interjected. "He's about to announce the new hunk."

"All the way from Jacksonville, North Carolina…"

"Jacksonville?" Hope directed her attention to the field.

"David Hoffman!"

The crowd cheered and Hope almost fainted.

"Did he say, 'David Hoffman'?"

"Yeah, why?"

"That's my boyfriend from Jacksonville. Remember, I told you guys about my folks running him off."

Red Braces blurted, "Get out of here!"

"Are you serious," said the boyfriend-having cheerleader. "Small world, huh?"

"Yeah."

"You going to talk to him after the game?"

"Of course."

~~~~~~~~

David's father had received orders to Beaufort days after Mark. Although his feelings for Hope hadn't changed, David felt it best not to pursue her after the relocation. The influences that interfered were still present, but once they reconnected, the romance was back on track.

David refused to tolerate the drama attached to Hope's newfound ego. His constant reality checks kept her grounded and focused.
~~~~~~~~

Because he loved Hope wholeheartedly, sex was not an option. Beaufort High had twenty-four pregnant ninth graders and they wanted nothing to do with parenthood. Hugs and kisses sufficed. On the surface, things were going well for the reunited couple.

"Hello, Mrs. Hoffman. May I please speak to David?"

"Hope?"

"Yes, ma'am?"

"What did I tell you about calling David? Back in my day, boys chased girls. We had a name for girls that chased boys and it wasn't a nice one, let me tell you. I already have one grandbaby on the way and I refuse to handle another."

"No ma'am. David and I don't do those things." Hope tried to stifle the tears, but they fell without restraint. "I'm not fast. I just really need to talk to David."

"Oh sweetie, I didn't mean to make you cry."

"Don't worry you didn't. I just found out that my parents are getting a divorce and we're moving back to Cincinnati."

"Ohio?"

"Yes, ma'am."

"Well that's not good. I'm sorry to hear that, sweetie. David is going to have a fit. Hold on I'll get him."

David picked up the phone.

"Hope?"

"I'm here."

"My mom told me about your parents. Is there anything I can do?"

"Can we go for a walk?"

"I'll be right over."

Twenty minutes later, David knocked on the door.

Sarah answered and invited David inside.

"Mommy, I'll be back before dinner."

"Where are you two...?" She looked at the sorrowful faces. "Just try to make it home before dark."

"I will. Love you, Mommy."

"Love you."

"See ya', Mrs. Tolliver."

"Bye, David."

They walked to the base pier and stayed until sunset. For at least an hour, not a word passed between them. David enveloped Hope in his arms and caressed her back as they cried. Overwhelmed by her parents' divorce, the source of Hope's tears was the realization of losing love, again.

"I love you, David."

David relaxed his tight hug and then pulled away. He lifted Hope's chin and looked into her eyes. After a sufficient pause, he acknowledged her confession. "Same here...I mean, I love you too, Hope. I feel such a connection to you. I don't know what I'll do when you leave." He turned away as tears rolled down his cheek. "I wish we could run away to Savannah."

Hope wiped his tears and then rested her head on his chest. "In our dreams that would be great, but it's not realistic." Her sobbing intensified. She reached in her purse for a tissue. "Help me understand how I'm supposed to go on without you."

"Let's not think about that right now."

Try as she might to honor their mutual promise to move on, Hope couldn't forget the special moments they shared; loving, yet innocent. Ripped apart by circumstances beyond their control, her feelings for David never completely dissipated. Another warped lesson in love established: never let anyone get too close because eventually they leave you one way or another.

"Dear God, how are You? It's been a while since I talked to You. It may appear as if I only come to You when I need something and I guess it's true. I got baptized when I was eight. Aren't You proud of me? The pastor said that I was a new creature and that old things had passed away. I was happy because I thought that meant that Daddy Jimmy would go away and he did. But now, You're getting rid of my daddy and I don't want him to leave. So please, God, help my parents work things out. I do not want to move or be raised without my dad. I like my friends and my house. And David, Lord You already know I love him. If You fix this, I promise I'll stop talking back to Mommy. Amen."

Chapter Four

Sin-Sin-nati

In less than thirty days, the carefree life as a military family was smothered by a new reality. Sarah had been a housewife for almost eleven years and now with provisions reduced to alimony and child support, the family was forced to live with Sarah's parents in Cincinnati, Ohio. For one long agonizing year, the Tolliver children endured a vicious cycle of rejection, instability and abuse.

Juggling the demands of five children, meager earnings and depression, Sarah targeted her frustration toward Hope. At fourteen, when a teenage girl needs her mother's wisdom and guidance most, Hope was bombarded with insults, profanity and an occasional slap in the face.

With her hands planted on her hips, Sarah stood at the bottom of the stairs. "Hope! Girl, you get down here right now!"

Hope ran to the top of the stairs. "Yes ma'am?"

"I said, 'Get down here right now!'" Sarah squared her shoulders, pointed to the floor.

Hope rushed down the stairs. "Yes ma'am?"

"How many times do I have to tell you to clean up behind the kids?" She motioned her arms like a magician's assistant revealing the reappearing audience member. "You can't even get one simple thing right?"

"But Momma I did clean up." Hope spanned the living room sprinkled with an occasional doll or Tonka truck. "They just messed it up again."

"You must think I'm crazy. I know good and well this room didn't just get like this."

"Then I can't explain what happened. I di---"

"Hope, why do you act so stupid?"

Hope shrugged, bowed her head.

"It's not cute at all." Sarah pointed to a misplaced stuffed animal for Hope to retrieve. "You know I went to high school with a girl who acted like an airhead. Actually she was smart but she pretended to be an airhead for attention." She spotted a stack of Leggos in the corner and nodded toward them. "Unfortunately because she was so ugly she didn't get the type of attention she wanted. In fact, people just felt sorry for her." Sarah ran her finger along the mantel and inspected it for dust. "She was the ugliest thing I ever saw. Real dark, with big bug eyes and buck teeth." She blew minute particles into the air. "You remind me of her."

Hope gathered the last of the toys as her mother smirked and then walked toward the kitchen.

"Turn on my girl, Natalie. I'm ready to dance to *I'm Catching Hell.*"

"Yes, ma'am."

Papa T, Sarah's father, walked in the house. "Baby girl, why you crying?"

Hope stood with the armful of toys. A baby doll fell to the floor and its leg popped off.

Papa T picked up the fragmented doll and reassembled

it. "You know that I can't stand to see you crying. Tell me what's wrong." He took some of the toys from Hope and placed them in the tattered cardboard box in the dining room.

Without looking up, Hope said, "Nothing."

"You may be able to get by with that answer with somebody else, but I know better." He hooked his arm with Hope's and escorted her to the front porch. He unfolded two faded lawn chairs and then motioned for Hope to sit. "Now I'm gonna ask you again and this time, you will answer me."

"Yes, sir." Hope sniffled to keep another tear from crawling down her cheek.

"Well."

Hope tapped her foot. "Momma said that I was ugly and stupid."

"She said what?" Papa T furrowed his brow and wrung his hands together. "You sure you heard her right?"

Hope bowed her head and nodded. "Yes, sir." Hope's foot tapping escalated to sixteen beats per measure.

"Guess she got tired of me getting on her for beating you, so she went for the tongue lashing instead." He expelled an extended sigh. "I'm not making excuses for her actions, but Grandma and I never talked to her like that so I don't understand where she gets it." He rubbed the back of his firstborn grandchild. "Your momma has a lot on her, but I know that she loves you, baby girl."

"She loves me her way and not how I need to be loved." Hope rubbed her hands along the aluminum armrests. "She almost beat me senseless with the tire tread she found on the side of the road just because I said 'what' instead of 'yes ma'am.'" Hope sobbed. "My classmates saw the whole thing when the school bus drove past. They still tease me about it." She shifted in the lawn chair to peel the vinyl from her legs and shake the memory. "The next day Momma told me how sorry she was and that she loved me. What kind of love is that?"

Papa T shook his head. "You have too much wisdom child."

"How's Grammy today?"

"'Bout the same. Doctor says she sits quiet all day because her mind is going away. She's in the early stages of Alzheimer's.

~ ~ ~ ~ ~ ~ ~ ~

Fifteen years after dropping out of college, Sarah completed her degree. She worked nights as an accountant for the IRS and slept all day. On weekends, she frequented clubs and then sang in the choir Sunday morning. Outside of the mistreatment, she had minimal interaction with her children. In a non-conventional way, Sarah taught her daughter responsibility. She succeeded in raising a scholastic overachiever however failed to develop a positive self-image in her child.

To ease the torment of periodic dances with depression, Hope experimented with alcohol. Despite the odds, she exceeded academic standards which afforded her the opportunity to attend a college-preparatory school.

Plunged into a world of affluent high school students, Hope fell from Miss Popularity to an inconspicuous wallflower. Her peers had expensive hobbies that ranged from European excursions during the summer to storing nose candy in the ashtrays of new sports cars.

She created an image to mask her pain and the bipolar defense diversified her extracurricular portfolio. Hope peeled herself from the wall. She engaged in sports, sang in the choir and acted in stage productions. Although her popularity grew, she didn't fit in with her well-to-do classmates. Her already troubled self-image plummeted into an abyss of insecurity, so she sought solace in bad boys.

Hope ignored the young men at her grandparents' church who expressed interest in her. She convinced herself that the church goers were boring, phony and not worth her time. The only nerdy guy that got Hope's attention was her best friend, André. He lived a couple of houses down from her grandparents and since André wasn't Hope's type, she expressed her feelings without fear of retaliation or rejection.

Whenever the doors of the church opened, André saved a seat for his esteemed ally. They often passed notes during service, but not even André's quick wit and humor could hold her interest past the choir's first selection.

She didn't have a personal relationship with God and as a result didn't know who she was in Him. She opted for guaranteed heartaches, rejection and dysfunction over men who even hinted they'd love her like Christ loved the church. However with the hurt of lost love ever present, Hope committed to her virginity. The resolve made break ups a lot less psychotic, once a guy's testosterone overpowered his patience.

~ ~ ~ ~ ~ ~ ~

A year later, Sarah saved enough money to get a place of her own. The move brought independence for Sarah, but yanked Hope from her only source of parental stability. The early-morning chats with Papa T helped to minimize the harsh words from her mother.

Although the move only took them a few miles away, the chasm in Hope's heart spanned deep into her soul. As her life spiraled out of control, she recalled the words of her grandfather, "God chose you out of the furnace of affliction."

Chapter Five

Tommy

Despite the drama at home and insecurities at school, Hope graduated from high school at seventeen. She believed that she knew all there was to know about men and life in general. Worldly, yet naïve.

Weeks after the commencement, Hope drove to a bakery to purchase a cake for her baby sister's birthday party. The small bakery, a local favorite for specialty breads, had a long line of customers. Hope peeked into the display case.

"They've got a German-chocolate cake." She looked around to see if anyone heard her and then she whispered, "Great." She took her place at the back of the line.

Three more customers entered the store.

I got here just in time.

One of the new customers pushed past Hope.

Hope curled her lip. "Excuse you."

Without a reply, he grabbed a number from the holder on the wall and then checked out the desserts.

"Aw, man. I didn't see those numbers."

The rude customer said, "Imagine that." He turned toward the display case and pointed. "I've wanted this cake all week."

"But that's the cake I was going to get and I was here before you."

He looked at the small placard. "My number is fifty-one. What's yours?" He smacked his lips as if he had consumed the last tantalizing piece of cake.

The lady behind the counter said, "Number forty-two."

A customer approached Hope. He took her hand, gazed into her eyes and said, "Honey, I forgot what we need. You go ahead and order." He handed the lady his number without turning away from Hope.

Flattered by the gentle hand strokes of the stranger, Hope said, "We need that German-chocolate cake, ma'am."

"Oh, you are so lucky. This is the last one."

Hope smiled and looked at the rude customer. "My, imagine that."

The considerate customer paid for the cake and, still holding her hand, escorted Hope outside.

"Thank you so much. It's my sister's birthday and she would have pitched a fit if I came home without her cake. She's such a brat." Hope smiled. "How much do I owe you?"

"Let me see. With tax and tip, you owe me… a date."

Hope laughed and twirled her hair. "No, seriously; how much do I owe you?"

"You owe me a date. You are gorgeous and I won't take 'no' for an answer."

"What if I already have a man?"

"Oh, well then I'll give you a few minutes to get rid of him."

His quick wit impressed her, his countenance wowed her but curiosity lured her.

"Okay. I'll go out with you, but only because you stuck it to that jerk in the bakery. Impressive." She nodded to emphasize her approval. "But when you called me 'honey' that was the icing on the cake."

"On the German-chocolate cake to be exact." They chuckled. "So what's your number?"

"What's your name?"

"Tommy; Tommy Tracy. And you?"

"Hope." She reached in her purse and pulled out a pen. "Give me your hand."

"You want to write your number on my hand? What kind of tacky stuff is that?"

"Maybe I have a strong desire to touch you."

Hope wrote her number on Tommy's hand. He called her and they went out that same night.

A well-intentioned guy, Tommy demanded perfection from himself and others. From his kempt hair to his pristine attire, he made sure that every detail was spit-shine polished. He mixed his favorite oils to customize his scent, but preferred the masculine aroma of Musk and Italian leather.

Hope admired Tommy's power. Strong willed; he spared nothing to get whatever he wanted. Even his forceful, fast-paced walk made her quiver. Over the next few months, he took the initiative to care for her every desire and she cherished his attention. She enjoyed having him select her clothes and instruct the beautician on how to cut and style her hair. His protectiveness catered to her insecurities. A match made in heaven; lived out on Earth.

Sarah knocked on Hope's bedroom door and then burst in without waiting for permission to enter.

Hope scoffed under her breath. "Whatever happened to

teenage privacy?"

"Your friend is in the front room."

"My friend?"

"Yeah, that Tommy guy. He looks pretty bad. You'd better get downstairs."

Hope bounded down the stairs to find Tommy shrouded in a hooded sweatshirt and sunglasses. Vain and quick to flash his handsome countenance, his attire signaled to Hope that something was wrong.

"Tom---"

He raised his hand to silence the interrogation, tugged on the drawstring to tighten the hood around his face. He grabbed Hope's hand, pulled her outside and motioned for her to get in the car. The tires screeched as Tommy sped down the street. He drove to a secluded area of Julienne Park. With the engine running, he locked the doors and then scoured the perimeter of the parking lot.

"Tommy, what's wrong? What's going on?"

"Nothing." He darted his eyes back and forth.

"Why are you lying to me? Your face is bleeding. What happened?" She reached over to wipe the blood from his brow.

"Nothing. I just…" He gripped the steering wheel of his 1985 Mustang SVO and stared out the windshield. "I got Tony involved in some mess and I don't know how to get him out."

Hope gasped and then threw her hand over her mouth.

"Do you believe that I love you, Hope?"

"Yes. Tommy, you're scaring me."

"Do you believe that I would never do anything to hurt you?"

"Yes, yes, Tommy. What is it?"

"I need your help, but I have to know that I can trust you. Can I trust you, baby?"

"Babe, you can trust me with your life. I trust you with mine."

He hugged Hope as if it were the last time he'd ever touch her. "That's my girl. I knew I could depend on you." He used his shirt sleeve to wipe his forehead, sighed, put the car in gear.

Fifteen minutes later, Tommy pulled up to a downtown office building. He sat in the car, murmured, said, "Just follow my lead."

Tommy got out of the car with his tough-boy gait; shoulders square, head erect, eyes confident and fierce. Hope followed a few steps behind with a more solemn posture. Two line-backer-sized goons were posted in the lobby like gargoyles. Tommy gave them the head nod and attempted to walk past.

"You know the procedure, Tommy Boy. Assume the position."

"Man, I'm cool. You think I'd come here with my girl and start some mess?"

"Assume the position."

Tommy lifted his hands above his head, planted his feet about a yard apart, huffed, "This ain't even necessary."

The second goon turned to Hope. "Your turn."

"You are not about to frisk me." She looked to Tommy for reassurance.

He mouthed trust me.

Hope submitted to the pat down.

"You're clean." He pointed to the elevator and then the gargoyles went back to their perch.

When the elevator doors closed, Hope blurted, "Tommy, what the ---"

"Shh, be cool." He shifted his eyes to the control panel, pretended to cough as he whispered, "They're watching us."

On the third floor, the elevator opened to a lavish office suite. A stone-laden waterfall cascaded into a pool filled with large colorful goldfish. Imported marble spanned the walls of the vestibule interrupted only by the dark cherry-wood receptionist desk.

Two more gargoyles approached the couple and another frisk ensued. A man in a custom-tailored suit seemed to appear from out of the wall. As the door closed behind him, Hope noticed that the inconspicuous threshold was flush with the marble.

"Well, Mr. Tracy, how is it that we find ourselves here again?" He took slow, intentional steps toward the fishpond. As he gazed into the water, he said "I gave you a break with the seven bills and now you're trying to bail on the two grand. Not gonna happen." He snapped his fingers and the gargoyles cracked their knuckles. "You've got seven days to get my money or I'll take payment out of your face and Tony's." He dipped his index finger in the pond, swirled it around.

Tommy bowed his head. "Mr. Carlisle, I don't have that kind of money. Is there ---"

"No more favors, Tommy Boy."

With his head still bowed, Tommy spoke to Hope from the corner of his mouth. "You got any money?"

Keeping her eyes on Mr. Carlisle and the goon squad, Hope said, "Are you serious? I don't have that kind of money on me."

"Not on you. Just do you have it?"

"I've got two thousand in my college savings."

"Can I have it?"

"But it's not enough and I don't get paid again until the fifteenth."

"I didn't ask for all the explanation. Can I have it?"

"Yes."

Tommy redirected his attention to the lender. "Mr. Carlisle, will you accept two thousand tomorrow and the balance in seven days?"

"As long as I have it all in seven days." He turned and disappeared into the wall.

Tommy and Hope exited the office building. "Hope, I am so sorry I dragged you into this."

"It's okay. I'm happy I could help. Next time tell me before someone splits your face open. I can't believe people really do stuff like that. I thought it was only in the movies."

"Trust me it will never happen again. I still can't believe you did that for me. I love you so much." He gave her a gentle kiss on the cheek. "And those guys," he mimicked a gorilla beating its chest. "Forget their faces. I wasn't too smart taking you there."

"What guys?"

"That's my girl. Your dad gave you that money for tuition didn't he?"

"Does it really matter? All I need to know is that you're safe. I can get the tuition back but I'd die if anything happened to you."

"I don't think anyone else would've done that for me. I really love you, Hope. I see us together forever."

"Forever is a long time, Tommy. Are you sure about

that?"

"Baby, you have no idea."

The not-so-dynamic duo crossed the busy downtown street. Tommy grabbed Hope, backed her into the dark corner of a business vestibule and shoved his tongue down her throat. Hope's body quivered with desire as thoughts of intimacy challenged her virginity. With a soft caress, she pulled back from Tommy.

He whispered, "You're right. This is not the place." He took Hope by the hand and led her to the car.

As Tommy jogged around to the driver's side, Hope sighed, satisfied that her chastity was safe. "Where are we going?"

"Got some things to take care of at my place then we can grab a bite to eat. You hungry?"

She giggled, "You already know."

Tommy sped to his apartment like a mad man on a mission. He flung open the passenger-side door and extended his hand to Hope. She riffled through her purse. "Come on, girl. Why are you moving so slow?"

"Just trying to get some gum. Dang. What's your hurry? The drive-thru window is open until two."

"I need you to pick up the pace. Got something I want to show you."

She zipped her purse without finding the gum and huffed as she got out of the car. "Whatever."

Inside the one-bedroom apartment, Tommy pointed to the couch. "Sit here for a second. I'll be right back." He darted off to the kitchen and returned in less than a minute. "What do you think of this?"

"A potpie?" She crinkled her nose and curled her top lip. "I thought we were grabbing some fast food."

"No, silly. Open it."

Hope noticed that the box had been opened and resealed. She peeled back the cardboard at the initial point of entry. "Oooo, it's beautiful." She peeked around Tommy. "You keep it in the freezer?"

"Yeah. It's my grandma's ring and she believed that diamonds are better served cold."

"I thought revenge was best when cold."

They laughed.

Tommy took the ring out of the box. He held it next to the table lamp to admire its beauty. "It's one carat surrounded by another carat of sapphire; Grandma's birthstone." He blew on the ring and then rubbed it on his shirt. "Look how it sparkles."

"It is a beautiful ring. Why do you have it?"

"I was Grandma's favorite so she left it to me when she died."

"Wow."

Tommy sat on the couch. "I had it appraised last year. It's worth almost ten grand."

"What?"

"Yeah, something about the designer's reputation for detail."

"And you're okay with keeping it in the freezer? Amazing."

"Hey, it worked for Grandma." He chuckled and dropped the ring on the floor. "Uh oh." He slid off the couch onto his knees.

Hope leaned forward. "You find it?"

He held the ring in the air. "Got it." He pretended to pull carpet fibers from the mounted jewels. "Hope?"

"Uh-huh."

"You know that I love you, right?"

"Of course I do."

Tommy ran his fingers through his wavy hair. "Grandma told me that I'd know when I've met the right girl. And…" He paused. "And that girl is you. Hope, will you marry me?"

Hope's eyes widened. "Oh, Tommy. I don't kn---"

"You don't what? We love each other and you've proven tonight that you have my back. So what's the problem?" He placed the ring on Hope's finger.

She lifted her hand to view its splendor. As she moved her hand to examine every facet, the magnificent piece refracted light that danced on the ceiling. After a sufficient pause, she said, "I accept."

Tommy stood and lifted his girl off the couch. He spun her around twice, laid her on the living room floor. He nibbled on her ear, whispered, "I love you, Hope."

Eighteen years of discipline and self-restraint vanished as they consummated the next level of their relationship.

~ ~ ~ ~ ~ ~ ~ ~

Early the next morning, Tommy rolled over and kissed his fiancé on the forehead. "Wake up, baby. I need your bank card and password."

Hope yawned, threw her hand over her mouth, cut her eyes at Tommy.

"Yep, your breath is slamming. You've got to work on that. You know how I am about odors."

With her hand still masking the offense of morning breath, Hope sat up in the bed. She pulled the cover up to her face and spoke from behind it like a veiled woman from India. "Give me a minute to freshen up and I'll get the money for you."

"No time for that. I need to get it right now. You don't trust me?" He looked at the stone that weighed down her ring finger. "Believe me, I'll be back. You owe me."

Hope raised her eye brows.

"Another round of loving before you leave for school."

Hope blushed. "Ten fifteen. The card is in my wallet."

"Your password is my birthday?"

She blushed again nodded.

Tommy kissed her exposed forehead, grabbed her purse, sprinted out the front door.

Two weeks later, Tommy repaid the loan to Hope. She figured he must have borrowed it from another female, but never questioned him about it. Hope's insecurity escalated to warp speed and she transformed into "crazy girl." Too immature to understand that sex goes beyond the physical act, Hope gave herself to Tommy and fortified the soul tie between them. In exchange, Tommy revealed more and more of his jealous and controlling ways.

"Girl, why are you tripping? The ladies have always pushed up on me." He raced his hands along both sides of his collar and then licked his lips. "You've never said anything before."

"It never bothered me before."

He smiled at the seductress in the Kenwood Mall food court. "I've gotta keep up my tough-guy image. Having you at my side makes me look weak."

Hope made eye contact with the tigress positioned like a predator ready to pounce on its prey and then snarled at her. "You used to hold my hand in public, but now you walk ahead of me. What's that about?"

He turned to face her. "I've been watching you in the

store windows. You're only one second behind me when you know you're supposed to be three. We've been through this before. I'm not understanding why you don't get that."

"I get it, Tommy. I just don't like it." She reached up to caress his face, but he stepped back. "See what I mean? My touch used to make you smile, but now you act like I disgust you."

He did a Michael Jackson spin followed by a slight hop and then walked away in the opposite direction.

Hope mumbled, "One thousand one, one thousand two, one thousand three."

~~~~~~~

Parked in front of Sarah's house, Tommy and Hope argued.

"I'll be back to pick you up at two."

"I don't need you to put me on a time clock. I can stay as long as I want. I do still live here."

"Two o'clock." He drummed his fingers along the steering wheel.

"You afraid I'm going to hook up with somebody? You sure don't have any faith in me."

"Two. Don't make me have to come inside to get you."

Hope got out the car and slammed the door. She stood on the curb and watched as Tommy sped away.

Sarah greeted Hope at the front door with a feather duster. She looked like a thin Aunt Jemima with her hair wrapped in a red scarf.

"Hi, Momma." Hope kissed her mother on the cheek, walked inside. She took off her jacket and dropped it on the couch.

"Wait just a minute. I know you see me in my cleaning
~~~~~~~

clothes. Hang up your jacket and grab the Windex."

"Yes, ma'am." Hope went into the kitchen, returned with an old tattered t-shirt and half a bottle of window cleaner.

"Small circles to avoid the streaks."

"I know, Mom. Wax on. Wax off."

"Oh, so we're a comedian now?"

"No. It's my way of making this dreadful chore fun." She bowed as if acknowledging a competitor and then posed like a martial art expert ready for hand-to-hand combat. "I pretend to be the Karate Kid in training."

"Whatever works. Saw you in the car. Were you guys arguing?"

"Yeah. We're always fighting about something." She sighed. "Women are so disrespectful. They'll see us together and still try to hand him their phone number."

"Hmm."

"And Tommy, with his flirtatious tail, doesn't deter the advances. He takes the numbers and then gives them to me to throw away."

"Well at least you know he's not keeping them."

"Yeah, when I'm with him. I'm sure he keeps 'em when I'm not there." She used her fingernail to scrape off a stubborn smudge on the window. "I'd feel a lot better if he'd tell the hussies that he was engaged."

Sarah fluttered the feather duster between the pictures on the mantle. "So you and Tommy are having sex, huh?"

Hope gasped. "Mother, why would you say that?"

"You think I was born last night? You've been messing with that Tommy character for almost a year and loved the fact that other girls saw you with him. Now out of the blue, it bothers you." Sarah sucked her teeth. "It's one of two things: he's cheated on you or you gave up the goody goo-goo."

Hope bowed her head.

"I knew it. If he were a cheater, you would have tried to defend your love for him," she smirked. "But since you tucked your head like a mongrel dog…" Sarah walked over to her daughter and lifted her chin. "When you lost your virginity to Tommy, you also lost trust in him."

"Is that why I feel so awful?"

Sarah nodded.

"He questions my every move and I do the same to him. I get worked up if he doesn't answer his phone right away and he won't let me do anything without his permission."

"You used to like his attention."

"It's gone beyond attention. He dictates everything to me and gets mad if I don't o... I mean do what he wants."

"Obey. You were going to say, 'obey.' He doesn't own you, Hope, but if you don't get this under control he will. I've been down this road; I know the signs."

"Tommy would never hit me or mistreat me. He's not that kind of guy."

"Do you hear what you're saying? I'm sure you haven't told me everything he's done but what you have told me is mistreatment. Get a grip, girl. Your first lover does not have to be your last love."

Hope bit her lip.

"What do you want to tell me?"

"What do you mean?"

"You just bit your lip. That means you're trying to figure out how to tell me something." Sarah shooed at dust particles that drifted in the air.

"I-I"

"Out with it. I've got things to do and they don't include listening to you stammer."

"I'm moving in with Tommy."

"Can't say I didn't see it coming. You sure you want to do that? If you think he's controlling now, wait until he has you under his roof."

Hope stared out the large picture window. "I'm sure."

"Doesn't sound like 'sure' to me. But since you want to be Ms. Grown Up, let me make this clear; I was forced to take care of you but I'm not taking care of your kids."

~~~~~~~~

The co-dependent couple had crazy fights about unproven infidelity inside and outside of the apartment. Albeit boisterous and unbearable, the neighbors were too afraid of Tommy to call the police.

His toxicity repelled and compelled her. Tommy's disturbed demeanor infuriated Hope, but his world revolved around her. With her personal image of beauty something close to nothing, she believed that she needed eye candy for validation. The bipolarity consumed her yet she refused to give him up.

Hope sat on the edge of the bed and admired her Adonis. He scoured inside his mouth and brushed his tongue so far back that he gagged. He trained his eyebrows to lay square and used spittle on stubborn stray hairs. He clipped and swabbed under his fingernails and then massaged his nail beds. The time and attention he gave to every detail of his appearance would have caused an outsider to question his masculinity. The routine made Hope evaluate her personal grooming. She stared at her hands in need of a manicure.
~~~~~~~~

"What do you think about me getting my hair and nails done today?"

Tommy primped in the bathroom mirror. "Sounds good."

"That's all you've got to say? You've been on me to take more pride in myself and that's all I get out of you?"

"I'm sorry, babe. Didn't mean to slight you. I've got a lot on my mind."

"Really? What?"

"I'm thinking about going to grad school. Got a meeting with the financial aid advisor today."

"Oh, well that's nice to know. When were you going to tell me your plans?"

"I didn't want to trouble you with it until I was sure I could make it happen."

"Uh-huh. So are you sure now?"

"'Bout seventy-five percent sure. I've been accepted. Just gotta work out the finances."

"Amazing."

"What?"

"I had no idea you applied, let alone got accepted. So what school will be favored with your magnificence?"

"Wright State."

"But that's an hour away. You couldn't go to Xavier or UC?"

"I'm going where I want to go."

"How long has this great plan been in motion and what female inspired you?"

"Come on, baby. You know you're the only one for me. Me leaving for school is for both of us."

"Uh-huh."

"Really. I'm ready to do the right thing. Get out of this

street life; use my degree to earn some legit money. I want to settle down with you and raise a family together."

"Yeah, right."

"Hope, I'm serious. I want more for us and graduate school will help get us there. I've wasted my folks' money long enough. It's time to put some action to my biological science."

"Oh, so playing the field is the new way to say 'advanced education'?"

"That's not fair. You need to accept the fact that you love a handsome man." Tommy flashed a grin and winked. "I can't control how the ladies come at me, but I can control how I respond."

"Tommy, you haven't shown any self-restraint and we live together. I can only imagine how controlled you'll be on campus." Hope turned away from Tommy and allowed the tears to fall. "It's my fault. I gave you all of me and lost myself in the process."

"Lost yourself? What are you talking about?"

"I bent all the rules. Gave up my dreams; my virtue. Put you before God. Everything I committed to do, I let go trying to make you love me. And for what? So you can move on to greener pastures filled with heifers and manure."

"You missed everything I said. I'm not---"

"Oh I heard you, but the carbon monoxide jumping off from your mess is choking me."

"It's like that?"

"Why play games? Why the soft close? You want to move on, so move on. Don't let me get in your way and don't get in mine. I love you but it's time for some fresh air." She took off the engagement ring, handed it to

Tommy.

"Girl, would you stop? Keep that ring. You are still my girl and we are getting married." He placed the ring back on her finger. "I'm going to work hard to show you that I'm committed to us." He pulled out his pant pockets so the linings hung like rabbit ears. "Nothing. No numbers, no names, nothing. I've been loyal to you, babe. Nothing else matters."

Hope swooned at his antics and accepted his promise of undying love. They retreated to the bedroom.

~ ~ ~ ~ ~ ~ ~

Hope stood on the sidewalk for twenty minutes after Tommy drove off for graduate school. She stared down the street hoping that he would come back to her. The assault of rain jogged her back to reality and camouflaged her tears.

When Tommy arrived on campus, he called Hope to let her know that he made it safely. He committed to nightly phone calls at nine o'clock.

"I'll stop whatever I'm doing to call you. It's my way of showing you that you are a priority to me. I miss you already." He kissed the receiver.

Hope sent a return smooch over the phone line.

"I want to bear the burden of proof, so don't call me. I'll call you. Agreed?"

"Agreed."

~ ~ ~ ~ ~ ~ ~

Distraught by his departure, Hope called Misha, Tommy's baby sister. Although Tommy tightened the reigns on Hope's friends and extracurricular activities, they had managed to develop a great relationship by telephone.

"Girl, would you quit all that fuss? He's just a man. You'll be okay."

"You don't understand, Mish. He's my everything."

"I understand all right. You made my brother— who ain't worth doo-doo on a stick—your world."

Hope chuckled. "You are so wrong for that."

"It may be wrong but it's true. Tell you what; now that Tommy is out of our hair, how about you come with me to church tomorrow?"

"I don't know. I've got a paper to finish."

"Girl, bye. You've been talking about getting to church and I've presented you with the opportunity. I'll be there at nine-thirty."

~ ~ ~ ~ ~ ~ ~

The storefront church was located in the middle of a quaint neighborhood. The coming and going of seasons had aged the bricks to a dusty brown. Bloomed flowers bounced around the small fenced yard. The stenciled sign in the front window read "Clothing Give Away This Friday."

As Hope and Misha entered the building, an older lady dressed in white from head to toe, handed them a fan. The organist rocked from side to side as he made the keys sing. The drummer whammed on the snares and tom-toms in time with the sway of the organist. The congregation of forty or so members stood in reverence to the Lord. Hands raised; voices loud; they worshipped.

"What you know about Jesus," the organist sang.

In unison the members replied, "He's all right."

The volley of lyrics prompted some to fall prostrate before the Lord. Others shook tambourines from hip to hand. A gray-haired gentleman with a slight limp stepped into the aisle and danced what looked like the Jitter Bug.

"Mish, what is going on? I've never seen people carry on like this in church."

"The Spirit of the Lord is here. When He touches you, you can't help but get excited."

"It looks like that lady over there is throwing a fit. Is she okay?"

"Yep. The Lord is working some stuff out of her." She patted Hope's shoulder. "She'll be just fine."

Elder Berger, the pastor of Holy Deliverance, rose from a refurbished chair. His crimson pastoral robe draped over his shoes as he floated to the podium.

"Turn with me to First Samuel chapter eight." He bowed his head and waited for the pages to stop rustling. He instructed the congregation to read the entire chapter out loud with him.

"The children of Israel petitioned Samuel for a king. They weren't satisfied with the judges the Lord had placed over them.

"The Lord warned them that a king would take their children and servants and put them to work. He would take their land and animals and use them for his own profit. And after he had stripped them of all they had, he would make them his slaves.

"Even with this admonition, the people told Samuel that they had good reason to request a king. They wanted to be like the other nations. They wanted a king to judge them. And lastly, they wanted a king to fight their battles."

Hope leaned over to Misha. "What in the world do the children of Israel and Samuel have to do with me?"

"Shhhh. Keep listening."

"The title of my message today is 'I Need a King Give Me a King'." He removed his collar and unfastened the top button of his robe. "It's gonna get hot in here." A slight grin creased the pastor's lips.

"Preach, Pastor!" A portly lady with a wide-brimmed hat flailed her hands in the air.

"Thank you, sis." He nodded in her direction. "Many of you are tired of being alone. You want a companion. You're tired of curling up with a pillow at night.

"I'm talking to you spiritual folks." He mimicked a woman and shifted his weight to his right hip. "Pastor, you just don't understand. I get into the Spirit, but the natural side of me needs a man."

"Understand this, my single brothers and sisters; humanity keeps you on the brink of insanity."

"All right now," Misha said.

"Shhhh. I can't hear him." Hope elbowed her pew partner.

"The children of Israel wanted what all the other nations had." Mimicking again, he continued, "I want to be married because Sally is married. I want a husband like Jane's husband." He sighed. "Always the bridesmaid never the bride."

More chuckles rose from the congregation.

"You want somebody to judge you. To make your decisions because you are tired of having to do it all by yourself. You want somebody to fight your battles. You want a man to go to work and pay the bills, fill the oil in the car and take out the trash. You're looking for a man to come riding in on a white horse and whisk you off your feet.

"Get over it! God said that when you choose a king,"

he pointed to the congregation. "He will mistreat you, dog you, steal from you, be selfish and have a concubine. That's right; he'll have some honey on the side."

"Ooo, no he didn't," the big-hat lady chimed.

Hope squirmed in her seat.

"After all the Lord had done for the children of Israel; delivered them from Pharaoh, let them cross the Red Sea on dry land, fed them angels' food in the wilderness, they had the nerve to ask for a king. He already had somebody lined up to be their King, but they were impatient.

"Y'all know the story. King after king mistreated God's chosen and left them with nothing. Your man will not be what you think. Why? Because you are asking for a king for the wrong reasons. You want someone to fill a void in your life. But you can't get a natural person to fill spiritual needs. You need an inside King. Call for the supernatural King. The King of kings.

"Let's look at verse eighteen again. The Lord knew that their kings would take them to hell and back. He knew that their lives would be turned upside down and inside out. He knew that they would crawl back to Him crying for help. Knowing all of this, He told them in so many words, too bad so sad."

Several people laughed. The fan lady bowed her head as her shoulders bobbed up and down.

"God won't hear you when you cry about the king you chose. Pleading 'that man you gave me' or 'that woman you gave me' won't matter to God. He wants you to have the king He chose for you. Your king was coming, but you couldn't wait. Now you're in a mess. So you try to be a rebel and break away from your kingdom to find another one." He put his hand to his forehead, as if to salute, and scanned the sanctuary. "Don't look at me like you don't understand. I'm talking about adultery and divorce.

"If you never deal with the inside issues, when your king comes you'll crucify him. Why? Because just like the Jews, you didn't recognize him as king. Let Jesus work out the issues in your life before you marry yourself to the wrong king."

On cue, the six-person choir bellowed several stanzas of *There is room at the cross for you.*

"Does anyone want to give their life to the Lord?"

A force tugged at Hope. She looked to see who had invaded her space.

"Late at night you cry yourself to sleep. The Lord wants to give you peace."

How does he know that? Another tug. *What is going on?*

"I know that someone out there is in need of prayer. Won't you come?"

Before she realized it, Hope had made her way into the aisle. Tears streamed down her face as she walked to the front of the church.

Elder Berger whispered in her ear. "Daughter, the Lord has heard your cries. He wants you to know that He loves you. Look to Jesus for love and stop seeking after the affection of men. He is your first love. Come back to your first love."

As the pastor laid hands on her forehead, he called for two mothers of the church. Both women touched Hope's stomach and back. They spoke an unknown tongue. Her knees buckled and she sank to the floor. The mothers continued to pray.

Sprawled out on the tiled floor, Hope had her most intimate encounter with the Lord. A consuming fire raged within and she was comforted with His peace.

The mothers and Misha escorted Hope to a small room in the back of the church.

"Honey, the Lord is doing a new thing in you. Do you believe that Jesus is your Savior and that He gave His life for you?"

"Yes ma'am," she replied, still a bit woozy from the experience.

"Praise the Lord," the trio exclaimed in unison.

~ ~ ~ ~ ~ ~ ~ ~

The inner peace equipped Hope to tolerate her Tommy situation. Although she was saved, he wasn't. She loved that man and held onto him with all that she had, but his last tryst was too close to home.

~ ~ ~ ~ ~ ~ ~ ~

For the first two weeks, Tommy called a couple of minutes before their appointed rendezvous time. But as the days crawled by, his calls came later and later. Three months into his relocation, Hope fell asleep next to the phone waiting for his call. When she woke the next morning, she called Misha.

"Why are you calling me? You should have called him."

"He asked me not to call him."

"Say what?"

"He wants to prove his commitment to the relationship and initiate the calls."

"And you believe that bull?"

"Uh, yeah. Why wouldn't I?"

"Duh, because he's a man. Call him."

"I will not."

"Call him."

"No. You didn't see his face when he promised to make me his priority. He meant it. You're not going to convince me that my man, your brother, is up to no good."

"Hope, because he is my brother, I know he's up to no good. Call him."

Hope ended the conversation with Misha and called Tommy's dorm room.

A sultry voice, echoed through the receiver. "Hello?"

"Oh, I'm sorry. I have the wrong number." Hope hung up, the phone and redialed.

The same voice chimed, "Hello?"

"Is this 513.555.1212?"

"Yes, it is."

"Hmm. Well can I speak to Tommy Tracy?"

"May I ask whose calling?"

"You can ask, but I'm not telling. Who are you?"

"One moment please." The line went silent.

Hope tapped her foot and rocked back and forth as she waited.

"Hello?"

"Tommy! Who in the… Who answered your phone?"

"Oh, hey. How are you?"

"She's still standing there listening, huh?"

"Now don't be silly."

"I love you, Tommy."

"Exactly. Me, too."

Hope slammed down the receiver. Fifteen minutes into a complete melt down, the phone rang.

"Babe, I am so sorry I didn't call yesterday."

Hope snorted to keep the nasal fluids from oozing. "I don't know why I even bothered to believe you." She smacked her forehead. "All the signs were there and I missed them; clouded by love."

"Look, I'm going to be honest with you. That girl was a study partner. We have an anatomy exam tomorrow and she knows this stuff better than anybody at school. Nothing happened."

"So why couldn't you tell me that you loved me?"

"Several of the guys were here studying too and I didn't want to come off as whipped. Honest, babe."

"Uh-huh. You got our picture up?"

"Of course. You took the time to have it mounted and framed and I have it on full display."

"So who do your study partners think I am? A cousin?"

"There you go. They know you're my girl."

"Then why the denial? It's not making sense to me and if it ain't making sense, it ain't right."

"I have enough stress on me with school. I've gotta maintain a B-average to keep this scholarship and I'm going to use all of my resources to make that happen." He paused. "Trying to call you every night is not working out. I missed one time and look what I get. I need my space. Let's take a break."

"A break? I haven't seen you in three months. You're all of an hour away and haven't made an attempt to come home a weekend or invite me up. You don't want a break, you want a break up. I'm done."

~ ~ ~ ~ ~ ~ ~ ~

To minimize the hurt of rejection, Hope took on a side hobby; drinking. She kept a bottle of Absolut Vodka next to her bed to thwart the night terrors. Her liquid diet between classes consisted of gin-in-a-flask. Invitations to Greek parties meant free alcohol all night and she accepted every offer.

Through her misery and depression, Hope maintained focus on academics. In her senior year of college, she managed to carry eighteen credit hours and work a full-time job. In the middle of her shift at Prudential Insurance, she stole away to the janitor's closet for a Tommy moment. She dropped to her knees as tears raced down her cheeks and pooled on the concrete floor.

"Lord, I know that I have disappointed You and I'm sorry. I didn't mean to make Tommy my king. I know that I'm being punished for my decision, but I never knew that love could hurt so bad." She grabbed a paper towel from the metal shelving unit, blew her nose. "The alcohol no longer covers the pain and my heavy heart can't take anymore. I'm ready to end it all and kill myself. God, please bring Tommy back to me. I don't want to die. I want to live and I want to live with Tommy."

~ ~ ~ ~ ~ ~ ~ ~

A few weeks later, halfway through her senior year, Tommy had a change of heart. He visited her dorm, wanted to pick up where they'd left off. He asked Hope to set a wedding date.

"Tommy, a few weeks ago I would've jumped on the chance to get back with you. I literally drank myself to a stupor and planned my death so I didn't leave a big mess for my mother to clean up." She paused to compose her emotions. "I even wrote a suicide note."

He rubbed her back. "Aw, Hope. I never stopped loving you."

"Tommy, you don't know how to love me." She moved away from his gentle caress. "I'm fed up with your lies and deceit. I'm done. You are not worth my peace of mind and you are most definitely not worth my soul."

"You can't just give up on us. You can't leave me!"

"I can do whatever I want to do. You did! You've had other love interests including Michelle." She cocked her head to the right, crossed her arms and waited for his reply. "Uh-huh. Didn't expect that did you?"

Tommy's bottom jaw went slack.

"Quiet as it's kept, I have friends at Wright State and they love to update me on your latest fling." She unfolded her arms and used the fingers on her right hand to tally the trollops. "Let's see, there was the tall model chick from Tennessee who loved Chinese food. The country bumpkin who could whip up some mean greens. The West Coast babe with the slim frame; she won the marathon." She rolled her eyes up and to the left to recall heifer number four. "Oh yeah, the nerd from Upstate New York you turned out. She had to drop out of school due to an emotional break down. And last but not least, the sweet-talking, phone-answering genius, Michelle."

"I-I ---"

"Don't try to deny it. I've heard all about your escapades from several different folks and their stories collaborate to the same conclusion: You are a *dog*!"

"I never messed with Michelle."

"That's all you've got to say for yourself?" She sucked her teeth and tightened her lips as if to hold back expletives.

"She spent the night because she had a long drive and it was the middle of the night."

"Tommy, what possessed your ex-girlfriend to drive two-hundred miles in the middle of the night?"

"She wanted to talk."

"Isn't that what phones are for?"

"I slept on the sofa. We didn't do anything. I swear!"

"That's not what I heard."

"Well I don't care what you heard or think. I did not sleep with her!"

"And that's the problem. At the very least, you should care what I think."

"You're going to believe what you want regardless of what I tell you, so why should I bother?"

"I don't know, Tommy. Why should you?"

"I did not sleep with her!"

"I'm sure you didn't sleep. She spent the night and I had to find out from your sister. If I hadn't confronted you, you would have never confessed."

"There's nothing to confess."

"You're trying to justify the unjustifiable. If you think so little of me that you could disrespect me to this degree, then we just need to move on." Hope shook her head in disgust. "I should've listened to Mish. She told me not to get involved with you."

"What is that supposed to mean?"

"Did I st-st-stutter? She warned me that you were not over Michelle, but I chose not to listen. I would've died for you. Oh wait a minute, I almost did."

"And I would die for you. I don't know why Michelle came. I told her not to."

"Why were you even keeping in touch with her? Maybe if you'd put some of that energy into communicating with me, we wouldn't be in this situation."

"Maybe I should be with her; at least she trusts me."

"How about you already have been with her? Why didn't you call her when you were in trouble with those thugs? I trusted you and you played me dirty." She glared at Tommy. "I guess we're seeing other people now."

"No, of course not. I don't understand you."

"I know you don't, Tommy. But understand this, I'm out!"

Aggravated to the nth degree, Hope called her voice of reason, André.

"Hey, Dré. You got a minute?"

"Sure what's up?"

"Tommy cheated on me," she paused to swallow the cries stuck in her throat. "I called off our engagement."

"Are you just speculating or did you bust him? Did he confess?"

"Some tramp answered his phone!"

"Okay so now what? Tommy is too controlling to just allow you to walk away. Why do you always attract the psychos?"

"I don't know. He wants us to be together and still see other people. I can't trust him."

"Men are faithful, trustworthy and honor their commitments. Tommy is not a man!" You need to come back to Papa T's church and get restored. Cling to God and leave Tommy alone."

"It's not that easy Dré. I can't fathom life without him."

Another Lonely Night
Where are we going?

What is this all for?
I give you all of me
Somehow you still want more
Ruthless women seem to come and go
But you say you're not to blame
I knew from the day you parted
We would never be the same
The rain outside falls faster and harder
As memories splash into my eye
Everything reminds me of you
It's so hard to say goodbye
You tell me you still love me
You tell me you still care
Yet when I'm alone and lonely
I call and you are not there
You tell me you still want me
That you dream of me at night
Yet dreams and wishes can't satisfy
My desire to be held tight
You said a day without my smile
Was like a day without the sun
Both exuded a remarkable shine
And yet there was only one
Well your clouds are blocking my sunshine
We're drifting further and further away
You can't just float out of my life
You promised me you'd stay

Chapter Six

Ryan

Hope tried to date other guys in college but Tommy continued to manipulate her emotions. He'd tell her he still loved and missed her to facilitate the notion that no one else could ever take her place. The truth was Tommy wasn't sure if he wanted her, but refused to let anyone else have her. Hope expressed to Tommy her desire to date someone new and then he'd make her feel guilty for calling off their engagement. Tommy, on the other hand, dated several girls to get over the pain Hope had inflicted on his heart. It took a few months for Hope to realize that she was being manipulated. Enlightened by the obvious double standard she found the courage to move on.

Late for a session with her study partner, Hope darted through the lobby of Apple Hall. She ran into a guy and her books fell to the floor.

"I am so sorry." Hope knelt to pick up her stuff.

"It's okay." He knelt to help her. "You pack a strong punch." He laughed, handed Hope her belongings. "My name is Ryan."

"Hi, Ryan. I'm Hope. Again, I am so sorry." She tapped the papers on the floor to align the edges. "I've never seen you around here before. Are you new on campus?

"Yeah. I transferred here from Alabama A & T to help out my brother."

"Is he ill?"

"No, he works for an advertising firm and they relocated him from Ohio on special assignment."

"You and your brother are close, huh?"

"Yeah, he raised me when our folks died."

"Wow." Hope put the last of the papers in her book bag. "That's what I get for not zipping this thing up. So how long will you guys be here?"

"Well it's supposed to be temporary but he just got a promotion. Looks like we'll be here for a while."

Ryan, an engineering major, waited with Hope. They engaged in a light, but philosophical conversation.

They met daily in Apple Hall for lunch and hung out between classes. Some days they listened to music and others they debated on world affairs. Ryan often talked about previous relationships which relieved Hope of the typical pressures of dating. She enjoyed kicking it with her newfound friend—no strings attached—and cherished his acceptance of her transparency.

The rigors of study often caused insomnia, so Hope called Ryan to ease her tension. Intoxicated by mere words, they tucked each other in over the phone lines.

"Hello, Ryan?"

"Hey, what's going on?"

"I can't sleep."

"So what's on your mind?"

"A million things; that's probably the reason I can't sleep."

"Quit biting your lips."

"How'd you know?"

"That's what you do when you're nervous. You're gonna make those sweet things chap. Are any of your thoughts about me?"

"Maybe a few. What made you ask me that?"

"I was just wondering. Do you ever think about why our life follows the order it does? I'm not gonna lie; I care for you. Maybe if we'd met earlier we'd be together."

"Earlier? You talk like I'm an old maid."

"You know what I mean. I just wish I could've met you before Tommy."

"Are you sure you aren't just saying that because I am somewhat attached to another man?"

"Yes, I'm sure. Why do you always question my intentions?"

"I don't know. I just think that if I were unattached, then you wouldn't be thinking about me. Men want what they can't have."

"You said for yourself that I'm not like most men and you are definitely not like most women. I would still think about you. Could you imagine if we were dating? Man, that would be so crazy."

"So how was school today?"

"The truth scared you so much you had to change the subject?"

"No, I just don't see where you are going with this. Don't get me wrong, I am overwhelmed by your honesty, but the strong like is destined to end." She yawned. "Sleep deprivation talking, right?"

"If that'll make you sleep better."

"I know we're tight now, but after we graduate, get jobs and marry; do you really think we'll even remain friends let alone be in a relationship?"

"Yeah, I think so. I honestly don't see how our feelings could change just because our titles do. Once you love someone, your feelings persist forever. Why do we have to marry other people? You can't see yourself married to me?"

"No, I can't. I know you a little too well."

"Good, that's what strong marriages are made of."

"How about I know you well enough to know the two of us would never work?"

"So what are you saying? You don't like me?"

"No, I love you but I don't think I could trust you in a marriage."

"Gotcha!"

"Got what?"

"You just admitted you loved me."

"So?"

"So, woman, you need to sit back, relax and let Big Daddy handle his business."

"So now you're Big Daddy?"

"You better recognize."

"Ryan, you are hilariously slap happy and so am I. Nighty night."

"What time is it?"

"Almost one and I have class tomorrow at eight. You do too."

"I know, but I could talk to you all night."

Hope yawned. "I'm sure you could but I'm falling asleep."

"Well take your groggy butt to sleep then. I see how you are. You used my conversation to make you sleepy, then after you're good and relaxed you want to go to bed on a brotha."

"Guilty as charged. I'll see you tomorrow I promise. Don't let the bed bugs bite and don't forget to say your prayers."

"Same to you, you little brat."

~ ~ ~ ~ ~ ~ ~ ~

Hope sat at a table with a few of her classmates. They ate cafeteria food and talked about the upcoming biology exam. Ryan interrupted.

"Excuse me, Hope. Can I talk to you for a minute?"

"Sure." She grabbed the apple from her tray. "I'll be back in a minute."

A nerdy classmate with braces and thick-lenses said, "Aw take your time, Hope. Take your time. That brotha is fine!"

"Did you see his abs and biceps bulging through his shirt?" another tablemate commented.

Hope rolled her eyes up, shook her head, bit her lip. She walked with Ryan toward a secluded hallway. Ryan bowed his head, leaned on the wall and rocked on the sides of his shoes. To get past the awkward silence, Hope gave him a gentle push on his shoulder.

"What's up?" She leaned on the wall to match his nonverbal stance and minimize barriers of communication.

"Nothing, what's good?"

"I was half asleep on the phone last night. Were we supposed to meet for lunch?"

"Nope. I was just wondering if we could hang out sometime."

"What are you talking about? We hang out all the time."

"I don't mean like that."

"Well, what exactly do you mean?" Hope stood erect and cocked her head to the left.

"I know you are sort of in a relationship and I'm not trying to infringe, but this 'just friends' stuff is not working for me. You're cool like one of the guys, but…" He lifted his head to look Hope in the eyes. "You are not one of the guys. You're a beautiful woman and I don't understand how your ex-fiancé—or whatever he is to you—could allow you to see other people. You are not disposable."

"Ryan, what are you---"

"No, please let me finish before I lose my nerve."

"By all means, continue."

"I consider myself an honest man and that includes the expression of my feelings. What I'm trying to say is… I yearn for more of you."

"You yearn for more what? You know my situation."

"Yeah, I know. But I can't seem to get you out of my head. I couldn't sleep last night from reminiscing about our conversation. It played over and over in my mind. I think about you all the time especially on weekends and it drives me crazy." He bowed his head again. "But if you're not feeling me, I won't waste anymore of your time."

"How are you gonna come at me like this, Ryan? I thought we were just friends."

"We are friends, but I'm having deeper feelings for you. And I think the feelings are mutual." He paused. "On a lighter note, I have tickets to see your favorite group on Saturday and I know you wanna go."

"You have tickets to see Outkast? You have stooped to a new level of dirty."

"I'm from the dirty dirty. What did you expect?"

"Humph. I'll go with you to the concert but no strings attached. Just friends, right?"

"Sure, whatever you say. Just be ready at seven."

"Oh, it's like that?"

"Thought you knew."

Although Tommy had given Hope his approval to see other people, she never expected to follow through. Ryan was cool to hang with as a playmate but she never thought of him as more than a friend. Low self-esteem convinced Hope that Ryan was too fine to be interested in her and only toyed with her to get to her diamond mine. If she knew her worth to God, she'd understand Ryan's attraction to her.

They enjoyed the concert and afterwards, Ryan treated her to dinner. Since they were just friends having a good time, Hope declined Ryan's invitation to come back to his place. When he pulled up to her apartment complex, she initiated the conversation.

"Thanks for taking me out, Ryan. I had a great time."

"You are more than welcome. So can I come up?"

"Dang! Are you always so blunt? I explained before that I'm not feeling you like that."

"No you didn't. In fact you told me you loved me. Did you not?"

"Is a platonic relationship going to be a problem for you? What exactly do you want from me?"

"I want you to stop pretending like you're not feeling me the way I'm feeling you. I know you believe you're with Tommy but newsflash, you're not. Where is he when you need to talk? Where is he when you're restless and can't sleep? Where is he when you just need to be loved?"

With each question, Ryan moved closer to Hope.

"Um … so I'll see you at school on Monday, right?"

"Aren't you going to invite me in?"

"Sure. Come up, but just for a minute." They took the steps to the third-floor apartment.

To avoid sending Ryan the wrong signals, Hope directed him away from the couch and motioned for him to sit at her dinette for two. "Can I get you anything?"

"No, I'm good."

She sat at the table. "You are still not getting any."

"Why do you say things like that?"

"Oh, you're free to say what's on your mind, but I can't? A candid woman intimidates you?"

"No, actually I find it stimulating. It's better than you changing the subject." He leaned over to kiss her, but she pulled away. "Girl, why do you keep playing me?"

"It's not intentional. I just don't understand why you want to be with me."

"Well understand this; you are beautiful and I want to be with you because I can't breathe without you."

Ryan kissed Hope ever so gently on her supple, yet tattered lips. Against her better judgment she yielded to his caress. After an intense excursion to Fornicators R Us, they engaged in conversation.

"Ryan, what just happened?"

"We just made love."

"So now you love me?"

"Yes, I love you. Despite your being a total enigma, I love you. One day you'll believe that."

"You know I still have Tommy."

"Then why are you here with me? If he is dumb enough to allow you to see other people, you are free to do whatever and whomever you want."

"I don't want Tommy to know about this."

"Why not?"

"He's crazy jealous and I can do without the drama."

"Yeah, yeah. This isn't about him. It's about you and me. So I'll see you tomorrow."

"You mean Monday?"

"No, I mean tomorrow. We're going out again."

"Is that your barbaric way of asking me out?"

"Call me Captain Caveman. See you at five."

Everyday with Ryan was a new excursion. Over the next three months, he obliged her whimsical persona and did whatever it took to make her smile. He exposed her to creative arts including plays, operas and galleries. He wooed her with rendezvous dates skating, dancing and skiing. He allowed her to shop on his seemingly unlimited charge card.

Hope loved Ryan's contrary personality. His refined and demure behavior complemented her gregarious nature. She countered his easy-going manners and allowed him to control the flow of the relationship. His conversation and philosophies stimulated her mind. His sensuality fulfilled Hope's need to feel desired. The reciprocal understanding kept them mesmerized and enthralled.

Night after night, they spent countless hours sharing the most intimate details. Ryan's ability to assess relational dynamics afforded Hope deeper insight into who she was and the motivation behind her actions. He knew her better than she knew herself. Absent a formal proclamation, they dated exclusively. Hope had developed yet another soul tie. Without warning she was obsessed with Ryan. He consumed her every thought and action. She contemplated his response before doing the simplest of tasks. She ignored the concerns of friends and family until an awakening graced her with its presence.

As Ryan walked Hope home after a romantic stroll through the park, she said, "Ryan, we need to talk."

"Sure what's up?"

"I can't see you anymore."

"Why? What's wrong? Is it Tommy? Because I can handle him."

"No, no it's not Tommy. I just need some space."

"Space is such a cliché. Keep it real, Hope. Is it your friends?"

"No, actually they are a little too fond of you."

"If it's your mom, then tell her I'm going to be an engineer. My potential salary should change her mind."

"No, it's not Mommy either."

"It can't be your dad because he said I was a man after his own heart."

"You're right; it's not Daddy either. It's just me." She bit her lip. "I can't see you anymore, okay?" Hope refused to look him in the eyes. His uncanny ability to read her would alert him that something was wrong.

"Okay, fine. I'm not going to push it. You know where to find me when..." The anguish in his voice made his words tremble. "Rather, if you change your mind." He shoved his hands in his pockets, walked away.

Hope went to her apartment and flopped on the bed. She toiled over her decision with intermittent bouts of crying and sobriety. After much thought, she decided to bargain with God.

"Dear Lord, I'm starting to realize how out of control I've become. But if You grace me with my period this one time, I promise I will never sleep with Ryan again. Amen."

Hope believed that God would grant her request so she sought a fresh start. Ryan however, wanted to hold on to the past. His random phone calls and casual visits turned into full-blown stalking. He demanded an explanation and late one night he called Hope.

"Hello?"

"Wow, you finally answered the phone. I know you've been screening my calls."

"Ryan, you sound weird. Are you drunk?"

"Maybe a little. Anyway can you come over? I just want to— I just want to talk. Okay?"

"I'm coming. You don't sound good."

Hope drove to Ryan's place and knocked on the door. When he didn't answer, she used her key.

"I've got to return this to Ryan tonight." She opened the door and walked into a dark room. "Ryan? Baby, where are you? Are you all right?" She turned on the lights and saw Ryan saunter into the room.

"I'm good. You look cute."

"Thanks. I'm not going to stay long. I just felt I owed you an explanation as to why things ended so abruptly."

"I'm listening. You want a beer?"

"You know I don't drink beer."

"That's right, you like that hard stuff. I got some Bacardi or you can have vodka; take your pick."

"No thanks. I don't want anything to drink. One of us needs to remain sober and clearly the one is not you."

"I'm not drunk I'm just a little buzzed."

"Well I hope you remember our conversation because I will not have the strength to say this again."

"I'm listening."

"I broke up with you because..." She fiddled with the hem of her shirt. "Well because I thought I was pregnant."

"And?"

"And I did not want to burden you with that kind of drama."

"What drama? How can you even equate a baby with drama?"

"Ryan, we've only been dating for a few months. There's so much we still don't know about each other."

"Obviously, if you thought I'd be burdened by our baby. It appears you don't know me at all."

"Okay, this isn't getting us anywhere. I think I'd better go."

"No, you sit your little butt down, look me in the eye and tell me you don't miss me."

"Ryan, please don't do this. You're drunk. You act like I enjoy being separated from you when you know I don't."

"Then why are we apart? I can't seem to get over you and that has never happened to me before. I don't know who you are anymore or what you've done to me but you have to come back. I told you that I can't breathe without you and I meant it. I miss you so much, Hope." Her name floated off his lips with a slight kiss at the end.

"Ooh, uh don't do that. You know it drives me crazy!"

"Then don't leave me."

"I promised God no more fornication."

"Who told you to talk to God?"

"Ryan, you're drunk and you sound foolish. I'm going

to go." She took the key off her ring. "Here." She threw it on the table and began to walk out.

"Wait, Hope. Just tell me you don't love me and I promise I'll let you go."

She talked over her shoulder, "I can't do that."

"Then how can you just walk away from me… from us? We are good together. What if we stop having sex?" He paused and looked up. "Never mind. That ain't gonna work."

"See there. And when I thought I was pregnant I realized that as much as I love you, you're not the one for me."

"How do you know you aren't the one for me?"

"I don't, but I still have Tommy."

"So you used me, huh? Is that all I was to you; payback for Tommy cheating on you?"

"No, I've fallen in love with you."

"Yeah, well I guess you should be getting home."

"Yes, I should. But first, can I have a kiss goodbye?"

"I don't know why I wasted my time with you."

"What? Don't say that. I'm still in love with you. I just can't be with you, if that makes any sense."

"It doesn't, but Hope, that's the bizarre manner in which you do things. An enigma. You claim to hate liars, but you're the worst type of liar—you lie to yourself."

"What are you talking about?"

"You pretend that all those steamy nights meant nothing but your body, heart—and above all your mind—told a different story. They all confirmed you loved me so much, it scared you! You were intimidated by our passion. No one had ever taken you to such an intense level before and you know that no one else ever will."

"Maybe so but that doesn't change the fact that I still have to go."

"Hope, just let me… Just one more time, please."

"You're right Ryan, you do scare me. I wish I knew how to say goodbye but I don't. I'm out."

Hope ran out of his home. What kind of attraction did they share? A relationship based on addiction and obsession? Ryan had a hold on Hope that she could not break. Voodoo. Just when she thought she was over him, he'd call and within minutes had her spellbound. With all the rejection she had endured and her insatiable need to be desired, seduction with words came easy. It was as if the devil himself whispered in her ear and told her everything she'd longed to hear. This warfare was not about Ryan and his feelings for Hope. It was a tactic to keep Hope distracted long enough to forfeit her destiny.

In the first trimester, Hope miscarried. She convinced herself that she had to shield Ryan from the pain she endured so she resolved to never tell him about the baby. It took Hope years to get over Ryan and even longer to break free from the bondage, pain and guilt produced from their soul tie.

Hope made it through the valley of despair. Many nights she didn't think she could go on and contemplated ending her life. In those times of desperation, the words from Elder Berger echoed, *Come back to your first love.*

Saturated in tears and confused about Ryan, Hope called Dré.

"Hello, ummm… Dré?"

"Yeah Hope, are you okay?"

"No, I need you," she let the last word trail for a couple of seconds.

"This is about a guy isn't it?"

"Yes," she whined, continued, "I thought Ryan was different. I allowed myself to trust him, Dré. I opened up to him. I exposed my true self and still got played."

"Hope, you need to trust God instead of trusting these guys with hidden agendas."

"If only I knew God like that."

"If you spent half the time getting to know God as you spend with these guys you would know Him."

"How do I spend time with God?"

"The same way you did with Ryan or Tommy. When you study God's Word, you are spending time with Him. You communicate with God every time you pray."

"I think I can do that. But what do I do when I yearn for the embrace of a strong, tall, virile man?"

"Cling to God. He knows your every desire. So pursue Him until you come to the divine realization that only God's mercy and grace can set you free from all past and present entanglements."

Hope received Dré's advice and gradually learned to love herself—flaws and all—when she saw herself through the eyes of God instead of man.

She spoke life to her situation and encouraged herself. She surrendered it all to God for He was the true lover of her soul. As He filled her with His glory, her desire for Ryan's acceptance and love waned. When she felt empty or tempted, she ran to God. Ryan was a lie from the pit of hell. God knew Hope better than any man and His love was unconditional!

<u>Let Him Go</u>

Letting go wasn't easy
Never thought it would be
Every time I closed my eyes
He was all that I could see
Tonight I made a vow
To release myself from his past
Hanging on to a relationship
We knew could not last
In time our wounds would heal
Allowing the residue to subside
Memories eventually would fade away
Restoration: the complete renewing of the mind
Giving my soul did not come easy
In return we'll make peace, I pray
Only time will truly tell
It seems nothing gold can stay!

Chapter Seven

Tommy

For the hundredth time, Hope told Tommy that the wedding was off and as predicted, Tommy didn't take the news well. He invited his family and friends to an engagement party and demanded that Hope not embarrass him with a no-show. Intent on ending the fiasco, she planned to use the face-to-face opportunity to let everyone know the real deal. She put on her favorite jeans, styled her hair to perfection and splashed on Beautiful by Este Lauder. She hopped in her Nissan 240X and turned the key.

"Come on, Betsy. Momma needs you to turn over." She patted the accelerator and tried again. "Please start. Please start." Nothing. "Okay, Lord. I guess You don't want me to go." Hope grabbed her purse and her books from the backseat. She walked to the library to study.

A few hours later, she returned to her off-campus apartment to find the red light flashing on her answering machine. She pushed the Play button.

The recorded voice said, "You have twenty-four messages. Message one."

"Hope where are you? It's about twenty minutes after six and you're not here."

Hope sucked her teeth, said, "Einstein," and then

deleted the message.

"Message two."

"I know you didn't forget. Call me and let me know where you are."

"Not there." She snickered.

"Message three."

"Hey, Hope, it's Tommy. Where are you?"

"Hey, Tommy, it's Hope. Not there. Duh!"

"Message four."

"Hope, you better be hurt or lying in a ditch somewhere. Call me or your mom or somebody you selfish, egocentric, wench."

By the time Hope got to the last message, she was everything but a child of the King. She called her mother to let her know that she was not bleeding out in a back alley.

"I probably should have called him but he needs to know how it feels to be ignored."

"You are something else. I can't believe you didn't bother to call him." Sarah laughed. "Taught you well."

"It wasn't my intention to leave him hanging, but obviously God had other plans for me."

"You leaning on the Lord now?"

"I always have. I'm just learning to trust Him, too."

"Well, Misha was the only one who defended you. All of Tommy's family and friends told him that he needed to move on because you had played him beyond forgiveness.

"I've been telling him for a while that we weren't getting married. He just won't accept it."

"It's hard to accept it when you keep dangling the prize in front him."

"I haven't dangled anything."

"When's the last time he tasted of the good wine?"

Hope paused and then swallowed hard. "A couple of days ago."

"Exactly. How is he supposed to move on and believe that it's over when you can't leave his lovin' alone? You're sending mixed signals and he's going to believe your actions over your words."

"Talk is cheap, huh?"

"Honey, talk is free. Integrity? Now that's costly. When you truly get fed up, you'll do what you've gotta do."

"I am done for real this time. I cannot—no, I will not tolerate his game playing anymore. I'm tired of the women he claims don't exist but when his phone rings, he answers quick and with a whisper. I'm tired of hearing that he can't make it this weekend. And my personal favorite: he was too tired from working in the lab to visit me. I deserve better."

Hopelessly Waiting for You
Diseased because I trusted you
An adversary in disguise.
Discarding Ryan
Was not a decision of the wise.
You soothed me with sincerity
So I chose to settle for less.
Plagued me with your grimy lies
That I utterly detest.
ANGRILY WAITING FOR YOU...
Desolate by the notion
You would caress my heart.
Endlessly be there for me

Promise a brand new start.
Now I've been infiltrated
And I can't seem to understand
Please disclose the answer
To my question of a real man.
DESPERATELY WAITING FOR YOU...
Feeble, I'd become afflicted
And my agony had no closure.
To love I'd become immune
Despite my abundant exposure.
You told me that you loved me
Fool heartedly I held my breath.
You were my drug
And I, a fiend,
It resulted in my slow death.
HOPELESSLY WAITING FOR YOU...

~~~~~~~

Every thirty minutes, Tommy called Hope. He left obscene messages with the receptionist at work and on her answering machine. After months of ignoring him, Hope accepted his call.

"I just want to prove to you that I'm a changed man."

"Tommy, I'm in no way interested in getting back with you. I have all the proof I need."

"Come on, baby. Ain't I at least worth a few minutes?"

Hope sighed. "If it means that you will stop bugging me, I'll meet with you."

"Great. You can come to my plac---"

"Sorry, dude. We're meeting in a public place."

"Dang. It's like that?"

"It's like that. I have a little time between meetings
~~~~~~~

today. Can you come downtown and meet me at work about four?"

"Yep."

Later that Friday afternoon, Tommy called Hope from the lobby phone.

"I'm downstairs."

"You okay? You sound agitated."

"No, no. I'm good. Come on down. I know you only have a few minutes." He cleared his throat hung up the phone.

With papers scattered across the desk, Hope grabbed her jacket and jetted down stairs. She spotted Tommy pacing the sidewalk next to his car and walked toward him. His unshaven face and scruffy mane caught Hope off guard.

"What's going on with you, Tommy?"

"Nothing. I'm good." He rubbed his hands together with enough fervor that had he had some flint, he would have started a fire.

"Doesn't look like 'nothing' to me." She rocked her head and adjusted the purse strap on her shoulder. "What do you have to tell me?"

"Get in the car."

"I will not."

"I said, 'get in the car.'" With a growl and grimace, he lunged at Hope and forced her in the car.

"Tommy, stop! What are you doing?"

He slammed the door. Hope tried to open the door as he ran around to the other side, but the handle had been broken. She slid to the driver's side as Tommy jumped in the car.

"Get back in your seat and buckle up. We're going for

a ride."

"Are you serious? Where are you taking me?"

He glared at Hope. "Don't say another word." He pulled back his jacket to expose a handgun. "Now slide over and buckle up!"

Hope obeyed his command. She stared out the window and tapped her foot. *Lord, please let somebody notice my car in the parking garage or that mess on my desk.*

An hour later, Tommy pulled up in front of his apartment. He grabbed Hope's hand. "Don't do anything stupid."

Afraid of retaliation, but more fearful of death, Hope resisted. "I'm not getting out of the car." She crossed her arms.

"Either you get out of this car or I'll bury you in it."

She succumbed. When they entered the apartment, the odor of worn and re-worn clothes, three-week-old pizza and pet urine infiltrated Hope's nostrils. She pinched her nose to block the stench.

Tommy pushed her into the bedroom. "Take off your clothes."

"Are you nuts? You brought me here against my will and now you think I---"

A demonic smirk crawled onto Tommy's face. "Take them off or I will do it for you!"

"Stop, Tommy. You're scaring me."

He grabbed the front of her blouse and pulled her to him. "I heard about you and that punk, Ryan." He snatched open her shirt, the buttons fell to the floor. "If you're going to have anybody's baby, it's going to be mine." He pushed her on the bed and ripped her skirt.

"No, Tommy! Please stop!" Hope cried and fought, but

the more she resisted, the rougher his assault.

Tommy climbed on top of her. "I'm going to get you pregnant and then you will have to marry me." He leaned down to kiss her.

She spit in his face, turned her head. "I still wouldn't marry you. Get off of me!"

He wiped the spit from his face and then slapped her. "I don't want to hurt you. Just cooperate."

"Tommy, stop! I am begging you."

Exhausted and paralyzed with fear, Hope could not move. Only Tommy and God know the rest.

After the traumatic encounter, Tommy bathed Hope and then dressed her in his clothes. He tossed her clothes in an alley dumpster.

"I told you, you belonged to me." He helped her into the car and then got in himself. "You said that the doctor told you couldn't have kids, but you got pregnant with that punk's baby, didn't you? How'd you manage that, you little whore?" He stared out the windshield and gripped the steering wheel. "That's okay because you are going to have my baby and we will be one big happy family. My family will be so proud." He looked at Hope. "You can't see that right now but I can. I don't know why you wanted to hurt me by allowing some man to touch what belonged to me, but I forgive you." He kissed the air.

Tommy drove Hope to her apartment. He helped her to her room, tucked her into bed, kissed her on the forehead.

"I'll see you tomorrow, baby." He left the room.

Unsettled, Hope balled up into the fetal position and rocked herself to sleep.

The next day, Hope called her friend and study buddy,

Jean.

Between sighs and sniffles, Hope said, "I need a ride to work. My car is there."

"Why is your car still at work?"

"It broke down."

"I don't mind taking you downtown, but you need to call the tow truck or a mechanic."

"Will you take me or not?"

"I'll be there in five."

Hope groaned as she sat in Jean's car.

"You look awful. What happened?"

"Nothing."

"I may not be a doctor yet, but I know what the wrong end of a fist looks like. Who did this to you?"

Hope told Jean about Tommy's latest escapade. Instead of the parking garage, Jean drove her to the police station. She sat with Hope as she pressed charges and initiated a restraining order. The officer instructed Hope to go to the hospital.

Weeks later, the results concluded that she had not contracted an STD; her period confirmed that she was not pregnant.

Come back to your first love, the small voice spoke.

The Cowardly Act

Violate me once, violate me twice
I never thought you could tell so many lies.
Lies to our families and to our friends
Inflicting raw pain that never ends.
Flowers no longer exist
A horrid stench fills the air.
Rainbows fade to black and white

My life seems so unfair.
What exactly was I thinking?
Allowing him to steal my hopes and dreams
I'd seen this movie before.
I'd memorized every scene
It was all a sick game to Tommy
And he played his cards quite well
He bluffed his way through the relationship
Then left the joker to tell.

~~~~~~~~

Hope sought solace in group therapy but rejected the pity-party mentality. Unwilling to deem herself a victim, she vowed to never let another human being—particularly a man—take advantage of her. Although her relationship with God had waivered, she knew that He wanted more for her. She recalled the Scripture about the enemy coming to steal, kill and destroy. She accepted that she must have something worthy of the enemy's devices and used that reasoning as empowerment.

She had spent the last five years in college to become a psychologist. She wanted to help troubled teens before they became her; however the rape brought her to an abrupt change of plans. She chose to work for the government, be licensed to carry a gun and blow away anyone who contemplated violating her.

A master's degree was required to be an FBI field agent. Hope couldn't afford to work on the advanced degree full time and didn't have the patience to put in four years as a part-time student.

The DEA offered her a position as a bilingual specialist because of her fluent Spanish. Daddy Mark
~~~~~~~~

cautioned her against it. He insisted that it was a death sentence because they wanted her undercover in Miami.

Hope's last option was to combine her bachelor's degree in psychology with a two-year military stint. Upon completion of service, she would receive a lateral transfer as an FBI field agent. She chose the United States Air Force and was accepted into the field of intelligence. The surprise behind curtain number three sent Hope into another tailspin.

<u>Rain on Me</u>

As the rain fell ever so gently, I set out for my voyage.
Rising with the strength of an eagle and the grace of a dove.
Soaring and dancing through the open field.
Increasingly attempting to keep the pace.
Faster and faster, harder and harder the rain pounded.
Drowning all sense of balance and stability.
I'd speed up nonetheless the rain hastily followed.
I surrendered.
And the sun,
Graced me with its presence.

Chapter Eight

Mica

Hope arrived at Lackland Training Base located in San Antonio, Texas. The facility ranked as the largest training wing in the Air Force. With a variety of training squadrons designed to accommodate one thousand trainees, the complex contained rows of identical brick and steel buildings.

Since Hope maintained a regular workout routine through college, she assumed training would be easy. She had heard the advertisements that boasted the military did more before six in the morning than most people do all day, but she thought it was a marketing ploy created by psych majors. Wrong. She stepped off the bus into hell.

Her degree equipped her to deal with the mind games played by officers, but the physical exercise and sleep deprivation almost killed her. Before the sun peeked over the horizon, the horrendous noise of *Reveille* jolted the troops from a not-so-peaceful sleep. In less than five minutes, soldiers were dressed with beds made to coin-toss perfection. While in formation, they sang the magnificent Air Force song, funky breath and all—no tooth brushing allowed until after the 0400 run. They ran three miles, returned to the dorms to shower, headed for breakfast before 0600.

Hope did not fit the mold of militia. Independent thinking and individuality were dirty words in the military. She used her creativity to devise ways to escape undesirable tasks.

On the third day of training, the instructor summoned Hope and Nicole Washington, a girl from her flight, to the office.

"You're being investigated for a higher security clearance."

Nicole stopped shuffling through the documents the instructor gave to her. "Higher than the intelligence training you secured for us?"

He nodded. "Do you have your parents' social security numbers, work addresses and phone numbers? That information is required to complete your background checks."

Hope said, "I don't."

Nicole concurred.

"Then call home and get it as soon as possible. When the authorization comes through, your files need to be complete."

Hope stood at attention. "Sir, I won't be able to obtain the necessary documents with one phone call home. It's going to take several calls to get everything you've requested."

"Very well, Airman Tolliver. Call home as often as you need to get your papers in order."

"Yes, sir."

Up to that point, phone calls were prohibited for enlisted personnel. Given Hope's liberal guidelines for phone privileges, she conjured up the need to acquire a lot of information.

Outcast
I am a blue car
Placed on a lot in the midst of yellows and greens
Thousands of cars yet...
Not one quite like me
They speak of our identical interiors
I listen but can't identify
I'd like to stick around and debate
But they are all automatic
Again I cannot relate!

The Air Force required strict adherence to the smallest detail, even the folding of T-shirts. Since Miss FBI-Field-Agent-to-be was far from domestic, she exited the dorm prior to inspections. Whenever Hope left her post to call home, the other airmen had to complete her work details.

The only detail Hope could not circumvent was dorm guard. Every airman pulled nightly guard duty at the dorm door. Uncle Sam didn't want perpetrators intruding while the flight slept. The mandatory assignment was scheduled on a rotational basis—no way around it. Hope improvised.

Hope developed manipulative tactics to acquire her desires and as it worked out, she managed to get two instructors on her team. On her first assignment as dorm guard, she caught one instructor coming in drunk. He entreated her to be his "new best friend." The other officer was a bit more difficult to influence until Hope observed him in a compromising hand-to-hand-combat position with a female subordinate who did not carry his last name. The cheating officer allowed Hope to sit in his office to listen to mixed tapes he had created. Since new recruits were not allowed to listen to music during training, this pass was valuable.

Each female flight had a companion brother flight. The companions did everything together except sleep, but when the female flight retired to the dorm, brother flight was in close proximity. The drunkard officer learned that a young man from brother flight liked Hope. He scheduled them for dorm guard at the same time and then granted them permission to go to the communal quarters or CQ. The small area—with a television, vending machines and phone—was reserved for ranking officers. Hope often enjoyed the amenities not afforded to other airmen.

Mica was Hope's friend from brother flight. He transferred from Five Towns College in Long Island, New York. Mica's methodical approach to life forced him to follow the rules. Even his confident gait—a military stride with a hint of brotha—seemed calculated. Hope often dreamed of her future husband. Albeit an attractive man, Mica didn't match her vision, but he helped her get through training and she enjoyed his company.

The companion flights wrote letters to each other—a bit strange since they rendezvoused on a regular basis—but proved to be a clever way to communicate in the restricted living environment. With similar religious convictions they didn't engage in sex, but the fatigue-scorching, shameless make-out sessions during dorm-guard duty came close.

The six–week training marched by in double time and graduation was less than two weeks away. Thanksgiving morning, airmen without plans for the holiday had the option of participating in a take-an-airman-home auction.

Residents of San Antonio, including professional ball players from the Spurs, provided dinner and a surrogate family. Airmen dressed in blues—formal Air Force attire—waited in the gymnasium for families to select them.

Hope rocked on the sides of her shoes and bit her lip, anxious to be selected to break bread with a baller. However, with a higher than normal turnout, families lined up on one side of the gym, airmen on the other, and the parties were partnered by single-file order.

Hope eyed her placement in the airmen line—about midway—and then looked at the other line to gauge her family for the day. Based on her estimate, she had a good chance of landing affluent dinner companions. The wife of one family carried her dog in a large YSL purse. When the miniature pooch peeked out of the purse, she stroked its head and tickled his neck. The glare from her gigantic diamond ring caused Hope to squint. The next family sported official NBA gear. Hope recognized the husband as a Spur, but couldn't recall his name. He wasn't a starting player, but a Spur nonetheless. The last potential candidates were a gothic-type family; pale skin, jet-black hair, tattoos and body piercings.

Hope mumbled under her breath, "Lord, please don't let me end up with those weirdoes. They're probably planning to serve me as the main course." She chuckled.

Minutes into the pairing process, the officer coordinating the Turkey-Day Waltz said, "We have more airmen than families, so we're asking each family to accept at least two airmen for dinner. If that's a problem, please see me immediately." No one complained and the two-step continued.

"Man, that throws off my count," Hope said.

A quiet girl from Hope's flight said, "Your count?"

"Yeah. I'm trying to see if I end up with Gene Simmons and family."

"That's so stupid," the shy girl said as she bowed her head. "I was thinking the same thing except I named them The Munsters."

They giggled.

Hope extended her hand. "Hi. I'm Hope. Hope Tolliver."

"Hi, Hope. My name is Sheila Withers." She gave Hope a strong handshake.

"Wow, Sheila. That's a powerful handshake. Didn't expect that from you."

"I may be tiny, but I can bring it if I have to." She avoided eye contact with Hope. "My folks kept me in martial arts and self-defense training."

"Really? What's your rank?"

"Master black belt."

"Well we've got to stick together. Looks like we're going to have the Simmons Munsters as our family."

"Okay. I'll take two and you take two. Deal?"

"Deal."

The Kung Fu twins were assigned to the weird family. A base commander walked into the gym. Hope recognized him as a friend of Daddy Mark. She grabbed Sheila's hand, turned to the Gothics, said, "We'll be right back."

She drug Sheila across the hardwood floors to Commander Jones.

"Excuse me, sir."

"Yes, Airman."

"You may recall my father, Mark Tolliver from Quantico, Virginia?"

"Yes, I do. How is he?"

"He's well, thank you." Hope cleared her throat. "We are grateful for the opportunity to spend our holiday away from home with a local family, but…" She paused to clear her throat again. "We've been assigned to a family we do not feel comfortable with." Hope nodded in the direction of Gene and crew. "Is it possible for a couple of guys from brother flight to join us?"

"I see. Well, as long as the family is receptive to having additional airmen, I don't have a problem with it."

"Thank you, sir."

Hope and Sheila traipsed back across the gym. Hope fabricated a story and convinced the Gothics to add two more to the chow line. One of the men from brother flight just happened to be Mica.

Hope leaned toward Mica and whispered, "What kind of screening does the base put these families through?"

"Judging from our bizarre family my guess would be none at all."

She elbowed him in the side. "I'm glad you're here."

"Me, too."

As the airmen crammed into the car, the Gothic son inquired about the type of music they wanted to hear.

Mica replied for the group. "We haven't been able to listen to music since we've been here." He looked at Hope, lowered his voice, said, "Well at least most of us." He smiled, continued at a more audible car-level volume. "So we're open to whatever you have."

He popped a cassette into a small boom box. *Check the Rhyme* by *A Tribe Called Quest* beamed through the portable speakers.

A grin spanned Hope's face. "That's one of my favorite rap groups."

Mica bobbed his head to the beat, "Mine, too."

"Get out."

"I'm serious."

Mica and Hope sang the lyrics word for word while the other two airmen stared out the windows.

The Simmons Munsters stopped at a grocery store. As the entry doors slid open, a row of wall-mounted payphones appeared. The airmen looked at each and then dashed to make collect calls like prisoners in lock up. Minutes into having the calls accepted, the airmen overhead each other's conversation and realized the topic was the same: the strange family. The group burst into laughter and then returned to chat with the person who agreed to pay the charge. Fifteen minutes later, the Gothics motioned for the airmen to return to the car.

When they pulled up to the house, Hope gasped. She threw her hand over her mouth to stifle the expletives fighting to escape. The four airmen looked at each other and then back at the Gothics' crypt. They hesitated to exit the car.

The house looked like a shortened double-wide trailer mounted on a slab of cinder blocks. Sections of the roof sagged due to missing or loose shingles. Globs of mud covered the porthole-size windows. A narrow path of smashed beer cans led toward the house. The airmen walked through two walls of grass and weeds like the children of Israel crossed the Red Sea.

Hope grabbed Mica's hand. "Did I just see a non-domesticated creature cut through that jungle?"

Mica chuckled. "It's only a field mouse."

"Only a ---. Boy, bye." She gripped him tighter.

"I do need this arm."

"Whatever."

Mica helped Hope up three rickety stairs that creaked under her weight. He opened the door that hung off the top hinge. The garbage-dump stench caused the airmen to step back. Yard-sale furniture and mountains of junk decorated the cluttered living room. The dining room was the size of an average family's bathroom—shower only, no bathtub. The table had an inch of crust build-up and a busted leg stabilized by flattened beer cans.

A mangy mongrel yapped and jumped on Hope. She squealed. Mica shoed away the hyperactive pest. It snarled, ran into the kitchen and then lapped up day-old scraps from the dishes stacked on the floor.

Hope crinkled her nose and rubbed her throat to encourage her breakfast to go back to her stomach. Given the circumstances, breakfast was going to be her only meal for the day so she needed to hold on to it.

The queen of the squalor approached Mica.

"Mica, you two are more than welcome to utilize our bedroom."

Mica and Hope looked at each, shrugged. They walked to the back of the home careful to avoid the doggy doo.

Hope grabbed four wet wipes from her purse. She handed two to Mica. "I can't believe they sent us in here to have sex."

"I know."

"I also can't get past how dirty this house is."

"They are poor, Hope. What did you expect?"

"Poor is not synonymous with filth, Mica. I expected

them to allow some rich family or better yet one of the Spurs to take us in instead." She huffed. "They robbed us of a real family."

"At least they're willing to share what little they do have. If more Spurs had showed up, you would of had a better chance at dinner with the rich and famous." He raised his brows and nodded. "Try to make the best of the situation. It is Thanksgiving, so be thankful for the little things—like not being alone today."

"I never thought about it like that."

"That's because you are a spoiled little brat." He mimicked Hope. "Excuse me, base commander who also happens to be my daddy's friend. Can I break the rules so I can be with my man?"

"That is not what I said."

"You might as well have, you brat."

"Okay I may have brat-like tendencies but who said you were my man?"

"I am, aren't I?"

"Well, let me think about it." Hope struck the Thinker pose and pretended to ponder. "I think you'll work."

"I know it sounds strange given we haven't known each other long, but I like you, Hope."

"I like you too, Mica."

"No, I like you a lot."

They kissed like the Frenchmen do.

"Wow. That was nice." She batted her eyelashes and twirled her hair. "I do have something to be thankful for."

"Oh, yeah? Let me hear it."

"I'm thankful that you are here with me because I could not deal with these people alone."

"Hope, quit talking about them and kiss me."

She obliged and then tried to unbutton Mica's pants.

He grabbed her hands and held them. "I'm thankful that we are not going to have sex in this place. That would just be wrong—wrong and nasty." He turned up his nose. "Besides, I love you too much to take advantage of you like that."

"Mica, are you serious or being sarcastic?"

"I'm serious. I love you, Hope."

"You're not just saying that to get some? You know, reverse psychology?"

"I do not play when it comes to love but I won't be taken for granted either."

"I would never do that. I love you, too."

Their Paris passion intensified.

"Hope, we need to stop." He kissed Hope's hand, escorted her to the living room.

The trash-heap king said, "You two didn't make much of a ruckus. You relieve yourselves okay?"

Mica smiled.

"Pa and I figured all that chemistry was gonna make you explode." She grinned and revealed half a mouth of teeth. "You dating exclusively?"

Mica said, "Yes, ma'am. We're getting married during our next base pass and you all are invited to the wedding."

Hope smiled. Her heart fluttered at the thought of marrying Mica, but her mind reminded her to proceed with caution. She liked Mica but didn't like feeling vulnerable. Their courtship had been brief yet intense like a bond formed during a crisis situation. Like strangers who comfort one another during a bank robbery, every emotion was amplified by the gnawing possibility that at any moment your life could end. Airmen often vanished some time between the morning run and lights out or attempted suicide because of the stress and rigors of training. Mica kept Hope encouraged and focused. He saw to it that she left the scene of the crime unscathed and whole. Hope fell for him and she fell with a thud.

Did he genuinely want to wait for sex or was he a master manipulator setting her up for an easy lay at a later date? With less than two weeks before they would have to part ways forever, Hope decided to stop analyzing Mica's motives and take him at face value. She allowed her feelings toward him to flourish knowing that nothing long-term would come of it. A masochist? No, she knew the pattern of rejection and had learned to embrace it.

~ ~ ~ ~ ~ ~ ~

On the day of their wedding—or rather base pass—Mica and Hope strolled the romantic River Walk in San Antonio. They talked and kissed as they enjoyed a candlelit dinner at an exquisite, Italian restaurant.

Sexually frustrated, the couple returned to the dorms. The drunk instructor was on duty. He motioned toward the CQ, turned his back to them.

Mica and Hope stayed up all night talking about their future together. When Natalie Cole's *I'm Catching Hell* came on the radio, Hope smiled.

"Why are you smiling?"

"My mother used to make me dance with her to this song whenever she was depressed. I thought I would hate it, but being here with you gives it new meaning."

Mica extended his hand to Hope. "May I have this dance?"

~ ~ ~ ~ ~ ~ ~

On graduation day, Hope had expected to shake herself

loose of Mica and start over at Goodfellow Air Force Base in San Angelo, Texas, but she couldn't focus her thoughts on anything other than him. The infatuation had progressed to deep emotional attachment.

How could I have fallen for him so quickly? Hope read the letters Mica had written to her every night for the last six weeks. The love notes contained intimate details of his life, dreams and aspirations. She shared her experiences with him.

Later that evening, the drunk instructor got creative to set the atmosphere for their last night together.

"Tolliver, Campbell, approach me front and center!" He held up Mica's blue dress shirt.

"Airman Tolliver, what is this?"

"It's a shirt, sir."

"No, airman. Lipstick; it's Airman Campbell's shirt with your lipstick all over it. How did it get there? What were you two doing? I'll tell you what you were doing. You were tonguing him down, weren't you Airman Tolliver?"

Hope's eyes widened as her jaw sank to the floor. She stood silent.

"Report to CQ immediately."

Hope ran downstairs before she burst out laughing. "He really sounded convincing."

Mica followed her and they hung out in CQ all night.

The next morning buses left as early as five o'clock. Hope's bus was scheduled to leave an hour before Mica's. He carried her bags, escorted her to her seat on the bus. While in uniform, they kissed; an unacceptable behavior. Hope looked up at Mica and his tears splashed on her cheek.

"Don't forget me, Mica."

He whispered in her ear, "I could never forget you. I love you, Hope. You are the only one for me."

The few emotions that Hope had managed to contain released at that moment. Her heart flooded with love for this man she had come to know as her best friend. After a lengthy embrace, she pulled herself away from his strong arms. They shared a gentle kiss and then Mica got off the bus. From the curb, he waved goodbye and blew a kiss.

The Fall
Easily I'd fallen
Delighted to leap for you.
I took no pleasure in knowing
Whatever he asked of me I would do.
Swiftly he caught me
Enabling me to catch my breath.
Sheltered me from the storm
Until all doubt had left.
Quickly he convinced me
Our intense feelings were true.
"Destiny brought us this far,
But love will bring me back to you."

Chapter Nine

Richard

Hope arrived in San Angelo, Texas where she'd been assigned for additional intelligence training. Mica weighed heavy on her mind. She moved through in-processing like a programmed robot oblivious to her surroundings.

At the brief orientation about the facility, the new supervisor caught her attention. As he conducted the session, he placed his hand on Hope. His attention remained fixated on the other airmen as he caressed her shoulder.

When he completed the orientation and instructed the students to leave, he massaged Hope's back with both hands. "If you need anything at all, don't hesitate to call me."

Hope grabbed her papers and scurried out of the room. "No he didn't just make a pass at me." Still reminiscent of Mica, she dismissed the advance.

Three weeks passed and the airmen were permitted to leave for the Christmas holiday. The night before airmen were scheduled to depart, Hope's supervisor invited her to attend a party at the Officer's Club. She talked it over with her roommate, Nicole.

"I'm not feeling his invite. I think he has an ulterior motive."

"Every man has a plan when it comes to a woman. Why does that surprise you?"

"I guess because I can't figure him out."

"You haven't even given him a chance. How can you figure him out without knowing anything about him? Osmosis?"

"Cute. So you think I should go?"

"Of course and I'm so concerned about your safety, that I should go as your body guard." The epitome of Nicole's free-spirited personality was to act without hesitation to do whatever her soul desired.

When they arrived at the party, Hope planted herself on the wall in the far corner. She didn't know anyone and wasn't up to mingling. Eager to leave, she pulled Nicole toward the door. At the threshold, their supervisor approached them.

"Hey, you. Glad you made it. Oh and I see you brought Nicole. Can I get you two something to drink?'"

Hope adjusted her skirt. "Sure, thank you."

He returned with two drinks. They sipped on bubbly as Hope scanned his body as if she had x-ray vision. Senior Master Sergeant Richard Donovan wore that tuxedo like a Chip and Dale dancer. Yummy.

"Where's your drink, Sergeant Donovan?"

"Oh, I uh…I don't drink anymore."

"That's great. But if you're not drinking, then why are we? Are you trying to take advantage of us?"

"Not at all, Hope. I just want you girls to relax. You look a little tense. And please, call me Richard." He took Hope's hand. "Come with me."

Nicole and Hope looked at each other and smirked. He introduced them to a number of his peers.

After a few minutes, the DJ played *Forever Mine* by the O Jays.

Nicole tapped Hope's shoulder, "Girl, that's my song." She stepped away and invited a complete stranger to dance.

"Don't hurt anybody." Surprised to be left alone with Richard still holding her hand, Hope stood perplexed.

"Would you like to dance?"

"Sure, I love this song."

They walked onto the illuminated dance floor. Their every step was in perfect syncopation. Hope couldn't place her finger on it, but she felt a bizarre familiarity between them.

"Richard, thank you for the dance but I have to go."

"Do you have to leave so soon?"

"Yes, I do. I'm a little tipsy and I'm afraid I might embarrass myself."

"Don't worry. I won't allow you to do that."

"That's sweet, but I need to get back to my dorm."

"At least wait for Nicole. Where is she anyway?"

"I don't know, but she's grown. I'm sure she's fine."

He scanned the room. "She's still dancing. Please allow me to see you back to your room."

"Thanks, but the cold air will do me good."

"At least tell Nicole that you're leaving."

"Yes, sir." Hope found Nicole hugged up in the corner bumping and grinding with an officer.

"You leaving already?"

"Yeah. Are you gonna be okay?"

"I'm good. See you when I get home."

"You are uh… coming home tonight, aren't you?"

"I will see you when I see you."

"Okay but give me old boy's drivers license."

"What?"

"I don't know this fool and neither do you." She extended her hand—palm up. "Give me his driver's license and I will leave your drunk butt with him. Otherwise, you can come back with me right now!"

When Nicole returned a few hours later, Hope returned her friend's license.

"You should've stayed. I had a ball."

"I started thinking about Campbell and wondering what he was doing."

"Give me a freaking break. I know what he isn't doing."

"What?"

"He's not sitting around thinking about you!"

"Nicole, that is so mean."

"I'm just keeping it real. If he was thinking about you, he'd be on the phone with you right now. But instead you're up listening to my crazy butt."

"So what do you think about Richard?"

"I think you're crazy to even contemplate messing with him. He is our supervisor."

"Do you think he likes me?"

"Heck yeah, but did you hear what I just said? Don't mess with him! It could go so wrong."

"Then what should I do about Mica?"

"What does your heart say?"

"My heart says it just doesn't want to be broken."

As they chatted about the night's events, they put up their hair and changed into their pajamas. They brushed their champagne-smothered teeth and then fell asleep.

The next day, Hope returned to Cincinnati for Christmas break. It didn't take long for her to realize that she hadn't missed much in her three-month absence. Hope had matured while her peers, whose activities and circle of friends had not changed, had no desire to progress. In addition to the disappointment of stagnated friends, Hope's thirst to see her family quenched in two days. She looked forward to returning to San Angelo.

A week later, Hope's flight left for Texas. At the arrival gate, she bumped into Richard. After several rejections to his offer to drive her to the base, she reluctantly accepted.

"So we meet again, huh, Airman Cinderella."

"Airman Cinderella? Are you referring to me?"

"I am. You did leave me at the ball."

Hope giggled at his corny line. "Sorry, I couldn't help but laugh. I really did enjoy myself."

"Then why did you leave so early?"

"I was feeling a little depressed and just wanted to be alone."

"Depressed? I have heard it all. Now I'm causing sistas to become depressed."

"No, I was just... I have a boyfriend and you make me miss him, that's all."

"Well I hope I can make you forget him."

"Are you always so forward?"

"You mean honest? Yes, I'd have to say that I am."

"Honesty is a good thing. Since you're being so honest exactly how many Hopes have you had at this base?"

"Did you just accuse me of being the base garden tool? I should kick you out of my car right now."

"That would be hard to explain to the base commander don't cha think?"

"Now you want to threaten me."

"That's my dorm over there."

"I know where you live, airman. It's my job to know."

"Good night, Sergeant Donovan."

"Good night, Airman Tolliver." He waved goodbye to Hope and then drove away.

Later that night, a ferocious knock banged on her door.

"Fall out!"

"Wh-what?" Hope thought she had escaped this basic-training crap. She stumbled to the door and peeked through the peephole. Just as she placed her face against the door, another series of loud knocks ensued. She jumped back and flung open the door.

"What the ---"

"Airman Tolliver, you are participating in a mandatory room check." Sergeant Donovan smirked as he searched the dorm room. "Carry on airmen." He exited and closed the door behind him.

Nicole rolled her eyes and then stomped off to bed.

Hope had a slight crush on Richard, but his late-night antics went overboard. Good-looking supervisor or not, Hope reminded herself that she was still in love with Mica and dismissed the notion of dating Richard.

Over the next few months, Hope spent a lot of time with Nicole. She witnessed her roommate manipulate men to get anything she desired; behavior one-John shy of prostitution. Still, Hope was fascinated by Nicole's power over men and the methodical process she endured to conquer them. Although each man was different, the outcomes were the same. Nicole intrigued them like a snake charmer to a cobra and men couldn't get enough of her.

A few days later, Hope received orders to undergo seven sleep studies. Bewildered about the tests, Hope questioned the base psychiatrist.

"Does everyone have to go through this type of testing for security clearance?"

The doctor sorted through papers strewn across his desk. "Uh, no, not everyone, however this process is standard protocol for a person in your situation."

"My what?"

"Airmen, I'm just doing my job."

"Which is?"

"Assessing your personality to determine governmental risks if your clearance is sustained."

"I'm not following you."

"As soon as the assessment is complete, we'll be able to address your concerns. Until then, you will comply with the process. Is that clear?"

"Sir, yes sir."

When Hope returned to her dorm, she told Nicole what happened.

Guilt shrouded Nicole. She shook her head and slumped her shoulders.

"What's up, Nicole?"

"I'm not feeling well. I'm going to bed." She began to walk away, talked over her shoulder, "Sorry 'bout your luck."

The next day, Sergeant Donovan called Hope to his office.

"Airman Tolliver, please take a seat."

"No thanks. I prefer to stand."

"Were you aware of the fact that you talk in your sleep?"

"No, I was not aware of that fact, sir." Hope assumed the attention position: head erect, shoulders square, legs shoulder-length apart, hands at her side.

"Let's start over. I have been instructed to disclose your sleep test results and clarify your options." He stood from behind his desk and walked toward Hope. "But before we get into that, you have to relax. Can I ask you a personal question?"

"Do I have a choice?"

"Of course, we always have choices. Who is Mica?"

"Excuse me?"

"During your sleep observation you kept moaning 'Ooh Mica…Yes Mica.' So naturally I am curious to know who Mica is or… was."

"Are you serious?"

"Yes I am. So, for the record, who is he?"

"He was…I mean, he is my boyfriend. Why? Does he affect whether I keep my clearance?"

"No, not at all, I just envy the man."

"You envy him? You are something else. Do you recall the first day I in-processed this base? You said that if I needed anything at all to let you know. Then you caressed my shoulder ever so gently…" Dreamy eyed, Hope reminisced.

"Hope. Hope!"

"Oh, sorry. You were hitting on me weren't you?"

He refused to confirm or deny her accusation.

"You had me going through all of those sleep tests to see if I moaned your name? Amazing."

"Don't flatter yourself." He walked back to his desk and picked up a manila folder. "Says here that your roommate failed her last exam because you talk in your sleep."

"Huh?"

"As you are aware, airmen must pass each of the ten block tests to complete intelligence training."

Hope nodded in agreement.

"Airmen Washington was called in by the instructors to see if her military career could be salvaged after she failed the exam for block eight. Upon questioning, she indicated that her focus was off because you kept her up all night talking."

Hope threw her hand over her mouth, reassumed the attentive stance. Nicole had unknowingly created a major situation for Hope. Because of the sensitive nature of security clearance, military protocol dictated that airmen could not talk in their sleep.

"I regret to inform you that the Air Force has opted to revoke your clearance on the grounds of a possible breach in security."

Hope's knees trembled, but she determined to stand her ground.

"The fact that you responded to questions while asleep, with great clarity nonetheless, poses a serious threat. As a result, you will be transferred to a new base."

"But I---"

"That's good news, airmen."

"How so, sir?"

"Because now we can see each other."

"I'm sorry, sir. I don't understand how one relates to the other."

"As your supervisor, I'm obligated to maintain a professional relationship. But when you transfer to a new base, we can do what we want, when we want. Unabridged fun."

"A free for all, sir?"

"Not at all. I know that you are a lady and as such, I will always respect you." He stood in front of her and caressed her arms. "How about I get your mind off of this matter and take you out for dinner tonight?"

"Sir, yes sir."

~ ~ ~ ~ ~ ~ ~

Richard took Hope on a typical first date: dinner and a movie. Hope saw the film as another whoa-is-me-and-my-girlfriends-who've-been-mistreated-by-selfish-egotistical-and-somewhat-unethical-men movie. On the ride to dinner, Richard gave Hope another spin on the movie. He enlightened her that three of the four women willingly engaged in adulterous relationships. From his perspective, the gold-digging, materialistic women baited the hook that caught them in the snare of despair.

After great conversation and a delectable meal, Richard pulled up in front of Hope's dorm in his Lexus. He had personalized license plates that read "Big Poppa"—a moniker from his father.

"Don't expect me to ever refer to you as big anything."

They sat in the car and listened to old school songs like *Devotion, Zoom* and *Between the Sheets*. Neither wanted the night to end but Hope had special duty early in the morning.

Richard walked her to the door, slobbed her down on the front stoop. Inappropriate for a first date, but Hope returned the favor. She kissed him with her eyes open and caught Nicole peeking through the blinds. She winked at her, thanked Richard for a lovely evening. She scrambled to open the door before he planted another unsolicited kiss.

Her dear roommate greeted her on the inside.

"What's up, hoochie mama?"

Hope laughed. "You tell me. I saw you watching us, you freak!"

Nicole smirked as Hope re-told the details of her date. "How's Campbell?"

"What? Who's Campbell?"

"The man you claimed you couldn't breathe without just a few days ago."

"You've got jokes, huh?"

Fine bottle of Wine
Like an angel engulfing a lonely soul
The clouds suspend in time.
Fruitful waters bring forth new fountains
My life, a fine bottle of wine.
Memories trickle down my face
Slipping in puddles of pain,
Releasing all the tears I've cried
Because every day it rained.
Compelled to permit him to love me
Love invited me to dinner and I dined.
Fruitful waters bring forth new fountains
His passion, a fine bottle of wine.
Thunderstorms and stormy weather

If only for a little while.
A profound purpose he had in my life
His mission was to see me smile.
And like the ocean, the sea and the shore
Endlessly he'd stay on my mind.
Fruitful waters bring forth new fountains
Our love, a fine bottle of wine.

Once the pursuit ensued, Hope learned a lot about Richard. The fact that he was ten years her senior, didn't concern her as much as the fact that he had an ex-wife and daughter.

"Aw, baby, you don't have to worry about her."

"I'm not worried. Just curious."

"She's remarried and lives in San Antonio."

"So how'd you meet?"

"Is this really necessary? You know you've got my heart."

"And now I want your story."

According to Richard, they were high school sweethearts who grew apart. Hope knew that he hadn't divulged all the details, but since it was his past, she basked in her blissful ignorance. It wasn't long before his past and their present collided.

Richard loved to make mixed tapes for Hope. He used the rhythmic lyrics to express his love and adoration for her and created romantic titles for each one. One day, he dropped off several tapes to Hope on his way to work.

She removed the rubber band that bound them together, spread them on the floor, closed her eyes to select a tape. "Let's see what we have here." She opened her eyes and read the title on the case. "'Remember How

It Used To Be!' Huh?" She popped it in the cassette player. The songs weren't the usual songs that made her heart flutter. This tape had a blues feel with songs about lost love. Lying on the living room floor with her chin cradled on her hands, she listened to the entire tape. The volume on the final song dropped and Richard's voice echoed through the tiny speakers.

"Gina, you know I love you. You know I would never do anything to hurt you. Please, Gina boo, let me come back home to you. I promise I'll make it right. Please."

"No he didn't!" Hope snatched the cassette out of the player. She didn't notice Gina's name scribbled all over it. Each 'i' was dotted with a heart. She called Richard.

"How dare you give me a tape you made for your ex!"

"What are you talking about, boo?"

"Is that your term of endearment when you're in trouble?"

"I'm not following."

"Hope boo. Baby boo. Gina boo!"

Richard paused. "Aw girl, stop tripping. I must've grabbed one of my brother's tapes. He's always whining to his girl to take him back."

"How do you know someone's begging on it?"

Another pause. "Uh because I know my brother. Hope, I swear that's not my tape."

"What's your ex-wife's name?"

"Camille."

Despite logic, his ex-factor bothered her. He had a connection with another woman that she didn't. She made every effort to accept his past while trying to intertwine their future but Hope was too insecure and far too jealous to acknowledge their affiliation.

Chapter Ten

Richard

One bright Saturday morning Richard called Hope to see if she wanted to go to the mall—peculiar as he detested shopping. Richard treated Hope to a pampering session which included her nails, hair and a one-hour full-body massage. She didn't know what prompted the lavish display of affection, but since gifts made her happy, she savored the moment.

Richard handed the sales associate his credit card. "Babe, I need to get my watch fixed."

In the midst of a buying frenzy, Hope completed her purchase, followed him to the jewelry store.

Hope meandered about the store admiring the splendor of gold and diamonds. Richard egged her over to the rings.

"You know you want to look at them. Go 'head."

She smiled. "I just love how they sparkle."

"Well if you had to pick one, which one would it be?"

She leaned over the glass display counter. "Hmm, that's a good question. Ooo, I like this one. No, this one." She pointed at a one-carat marquis-cut diamond solitaire.

The sales associate slid open the display door and handed Hope the ring. "Would you like to try it on, ma'am?"

"No thank you. I'm just looking while he gets his watch fixed." She moved to the next display case.

Richard nodded to the associate to hand him the ring. "Hope."

"Yes," she said as she continued to look at the jewelry.

"Hope."

She took a couple of steps back while gazing into the display case. In a somewhat agitated tone, she said, "Yes?"

"Hope!"

"What?!" She looked up and then bowed her head to see Richard on bended knee.

With his head low, he presented the ring to Hope. "Will you marry me?" He lifted his head.

She stared at Richard and the beautiful ring. Their brief, yet intense, courtship was far from ready-for-marriage status. He'd never met her family nor had she met his. He was fine, cultured and well-educated, with a great sense of humor, so why the unprovoked act of desperation?

She recalled a situation from three weeks earlier. Following the love-ballad incident, Hope put on her super-sleuth hat and snooped around Richard's office. Although she didn't find any evidence incriminating him of infidelity, she did find copies of denied orders. In bold red letters, the document was stamped, "Second set of orders. First orders declined." Richard had not presented Hope with all of her you-can't-work-in-intelligence options. She could have separated from the Air Force because her original contract was breached. She had the option to receive orders to Wright Patterson Air Force

Base in the hospital's psychiatric department. Wright Patterson was an hour from Cincinnati and psychology was her major. A perfect fit. But instead of being forthright, Richard wore the manipulative hat and led her to believe that her only option was to transfer.

Comments from strangers pierced Hope's silence.

"Maybe she's not ready."

"Give her more time with less pressure."

"Well answer him already."

"What is she waiting for?"

With a sexy, country twang, Richard said, "Well baby?"

"I'm not ready for marriage. I'm too young. I look forward to marrying you in the future…" She looked at the 14K gold ring. "The near future. So I guess my answer is yes!"

"You guess? I need you to know!"

Hope screamed. "Yes, I… I want to marry you Richard!"

~~~~~~~~

Wedding planning topped Richard's priority list. Without delay, he registered for marital counseling—a prerequisite at his church. The class was intended to enlighten couples about the true purpose of covenant thus reducing the possibility of divorce. The first day of class accomplished its goal.

Spending forever with anyone, especially Richard, terrified Hope, but until she had a better plan, she maintained the appearance of a happy fiancé. Although she wasn't equipped for marriage, she wasn't prepared to lose him either.
~~~~~~~~

"Dear God, Richard attends church faithfully, but does he have a true relationship with You? Whether he does or not, I want to know You better. I accepted his marriage proposal, but if he's not from You, please show me. Amen."

Hope's heart replied, *Come back to your first love.*

~ ~ ~ ~ ~ ~ ~

To consummate their engagement, Richard asked Hope on a Mexican vacation. She had already committed to helping Nicole celebrate her birthday that same week, but to keep up the masquerade, she agreed. She apologized to Nicole, who graciously accepted the cancellation, and then went back to the charade.

The morning of their departure to Cancun, Hope double-checked her suitcase. As she added a couple of her unmentionables, the phone rang.

Richard chimed through the receiver. "Hey baby, are you ready to go?"

"You know it. Where are you? We need to be at the airport soon and you know punctuality is my solace."

"That's just it. I have to get my daughter from San Antonio today so I can't make it. But you go and try to have fun without me."

"Richard, are you serious? You didn't know that you had to get your daughter before this morning? Are you trying to play me dirty?"

"Naw, baby, nothing like that. I promise. Don't you trust me?"

"Nope, I pretty much don't trust a man until he gives me a reason to and your poor planning is not pleading your case. You expect me to go out of the country while you do who knows what. More importantly, today is

Nicole's birthday, remember? So I gave up plans with her just so you could bail on me."

"You know how important my daughter is to me. Please don't be that way. I love you."

She swooned. "Okay." The 'l' word did it for her. She looked at the over-sized rock on her finger, exhaled. The makings of a gold digger? Perhaps Hope was Nicole's protégé after all.

She went on the expense-free trip to Mexico, unaccompanied, returned frustrated. She had no way to check up on Richard's whereabouts and like sand that drops through an hour glass, her trust in him dwindled. She caught a cab from the airport and as soon as she walked in the dorm, the phone shrilled.

"Hey baby, are you awake?"

"Yeah, I'm just getting in. The flight was delayed a few hours." She dropped her bags. "I missed you something awful."

"I missed you too, baby. Why don't you come over?"

"You want me to come over tonight?

"Yes."

"I don't think so. It's way too late."

"Then sleep over."

This man had never asked Hope to spend the night. Did he miss her or was he feeling guilty about cheating on her with some nasty girl while she kicked up sand on the Mexican beaches? Why had they never made love? Was Richard abstinent because fornication was a sin or did another woman have his heart?

"I don't think that'd be wise. We've been so good about abstaining and I don't want to tempt you."

"Are you saying we can't spend the night together

without having sex?"

"Yes."

"Hope, please come over. Everything will be fine. Trust me."

Like that's a new one, Hope thought and rolled her eyes. Who was she trying to fool? She was miserable without Richard and longed to have his muscular body pressed against hers, but she stood her ground. Who knew what he'd been doing the past few days? And she refused to accommodate his desires.

Twenty minutes later Hope arrived at Richard's house with her overnight bag. The throbbing that welled within her negated her commitment to chastity.

Although it had been less than a week since she last saw him, Richard looked more defined. Hope swore she counted an eight-pack abs. She yearned for him, but determined to not initiate an encounter. The effort she made to drive to his place was clue enough of her expectations.

They chatted briefly, watched a little television and prepared for bed. He offered to sleep on the sofa but Hope insisted that he sleep in the bed with her. Whether sleep deprivation or divine intervention, the couple fell asleep.

The following morning as they prepared for work, Hope noticed a change in Richard's disposition. He went from loving and affectionate to distant and unattached.

When they arrived at work, Richard lagged behind at the car. Since Richard was no longer Hope's supervisor, dating was permitted, however, he refused to expose their relationship. Hope accommodated his wishes.

"Can't appear weak," he told her.

They worked in adjacent offices yet avoided eating

lunch together. On the occasions their paths crossed, Richard offered a nonchalant greeting much like a simple salutation to a stranger.

He tried to hide quick glances toward her. His poker face diminished and a slight smile creased his lips. His pronounced cadence shifted to a light gait and he often hummed when he saw her. No one in the office was fooled by his antics.

Dear God, I've been reading Your Word and trying to make better decisions. However, lately this new man has made me so confused. I think he's really sweet plus I don't want to mess things up. So Lord, please help me to hold out until I'm married. I want to do things the right way. You are always looking out for me so I know You will lead and guide me in the right direction. Thank You, Father God. Amen.

~~~~~~~

April brought turbulent showers that twisted into a raging storm. Richard received orders to Kunsan, Air Force Base in Korea. Although they were active duty, Hope never anticipated them being separated by orders to different bases. She heard the buzz around the office all day, but nothing from Richard. Just before lunch, he slipped her a note. They left work early to run back to his place. Richard ordered Chinese and suggested they talk before the food arrived.

"I'm sure you've heard, but I want you to hear it from me. I received orders overseas."

"I know."

"The good news is that I don't leave until December."

"So what's the bad news?"

"I have to leave. Since we're only engaged, the Air
~~~~~~~

Force is not required to match our assignments."

"So what am I supposed to do?"

"I want you to request to be sent to Kunsan. I'll take it from there."

"What are you talking about Richard? If I could receive orders that easily, why have I been waiting all of this time?"

"I know orders are available for your rank, but I don't know what career field they would reclassify you into."

"Are you sure you don't know Richard? Keep it real."

"You want me to be real?"

"No, please lie to me. Isn't that what made your ex stick around?" She rapped her fingers along the couch seat cushion. *Did I just say that out loud?*

"You never cease to amaze me. I have tried my best to make you feel secure but you doubt anything positive I say about you. You act like you're not worthy to be loved and I don't understand how you can't see your worth. Why won't you allow me love you?"

Hope cried. "Richard, one minute you're open and honest and the next minute you're vague and evasive. How can such diverse personalities co-exist?"

His silence was interrupted by the chime of the doorbell. Richard paid the delivery guy, set the food on the table and blessed it. They ate in silence, until Hope began to cry.

"I'm going back to base tonight," she said as she placed the chopsticks in the empty white to-go box. She swiped at the tears, stood, gathered her belongings.

"Hope, don't cry. I can't let you leave like this. Stay the night and we'll ride in together in the morning."

"You don't care about me."

"Yes I do. Baby, what do you want from me?"

Hope dropped her keys, purse and jacket on the floor. She ran to Richard and kissed him with pent-up passion. He wiped her tears with a napkin from Tae Pings, carried her to his bedroom. Hope exhaled as he gently placed her on his bed. He removed each article of clothing from Hope's voluptuous yet petite body. As Richard penetrated the inner depths of Hope's soul with intense, sweltering fire, the unadulterated elation was a type of hell.

"Hope, I'm going to call the base and tell them we won't be returning this afternoon because something came up."

Hope giggled. "Yeah, something came up all right."

"Do you think you can be with me and only me forever?"

"Why disturb the mood with such a question?"

"You don't trust me, do you?"

"I trusted you to refrain from making love to me but you see what just happened."

"You are driving me crazy! I love you, so I refuse to apologize for making love to you."

"I love you, too, but we're not married. You were supposed to love me enough to wait. Instead of creating true covenant with God, we created a soul tie."

"God knows our hearts."

"Stop twisting Scripture. I'm not where I need to be in God but I know that is not what He meant. Religious Christians drive me nuts with their duplicity."

The next morning Hope drove back to work. She received orders to Kunsan. She initially submitted her acceptance then later retracted it. She wasn't ready for marriage, but if she followed Richard to Kunsan, marriage was inevitable. Turning down the orders was easy; Richard's reaction was a bit more complicated. Panic-stricken, he summoned Hope.

"Airman Tolliver!"

"Yes, sir. Is there a problem?"

"Have a seat please and close the door."

Hope sighed, plopped onto the chair. "Okay Richard cut the crap. Say what you have to say."

"I don't know how to inquire politely so let me just put it out there. Why did you turn down your orders to Kunsan?"

"Why didn't you tell me I had orders to Wright Patt or that I was permitted to separate from the Air Force? Why didn't you tell me you were making decisions on my behalf that weren't your decisions to make?"

"Is that what you think?"

"No, Richard, that's what I know!"

"So that's what this is all about? Are you trying to teach me a lesson?"

"I'm sorry but I can't teach you integrity. My daddy taught me that if you know something is wrong, don't do it. You don't intentionally deceive people you claim to love. I'm out of here." Hope grabbed her things and began to walk out.

Richard grabbed her arm, whispered in her ear. "Where exactly do you think you're going," he raised his voice. "You have plenty of work to do. You called in yesterday, remember?"

"No, you called in for me. Don't you remember? You take care of the work since you love taking care of things for me."

In less than three days, Hope received orders to

Wichita Falls, Texas. She was scheduled to leave in three weeks, but she distanced herself from Richard immediately. She was in love with him, but she loved Mica, so she did what she did best: fled.

Hope returned to her dorm. Nicole informed her that she was annoyed by Richard's incessant phone calls. Upon the next incoming call, Hope refused to speak to him. She had made a mess of things and needed time to work through the chaos. If only she'd been honest and rejected his proposal.

"Nicole, what am I going to do?"

"I don't know. You sound like you really love this man. Do you?"

"You know I do."

"Dear child, I taught you better than to get caught up. You have Mica over here thinking you love him while Richard remains dazed and confused."

"Poor, Richard. What did I get him into?"

"Don't feel bad. I doubt you're the first airman he's done this to and probably won't be the last."

"You really think he's done this before?"

"Girl, please! What have you done in a short period of time that was so off the chain that he felt the excessive need to marry you?" She laughed.

"Do you think he's proposed to other airmen, too?"

"Oh, I forgot about that. Maybe he really does love you. Heck, I need you to teach a sista a few tricks."

"That's not funny, Nicole. I really do love him."

"Aw how cute. You love him and he loves your goodies."

"No, that's where you're wrong. We've only slept together once and that was just the other night. It felt heavenly but this bondage is like I'm trapped in hell."

"I'm stuck on the only-had-sex-once statement. Are you telling me the truth?"

"I promise."

"Okay, kryptonite."

"He wants me to come over tonight. Do you think I should go?"

"Like it matters what I think. You're gonna do what you're gonna do. So go if you want to."

Hope rehearsed her monologue as she sped to his house. She rang the doorbell, had second thoughts, turned to walk away. Richard inched the door open enough to peak his head through.

"Where are you vanishing to now?"

Hope turned toward him. "Hi, umm can I come in?"

He shifted his eyes to the right, lowered his voice. "Not right now, I have company."

Hope barged inside the house. She yelled and screamed as she searched from one room to the next.

Richard sat on the couch, leaned back, crossed his legs. He laughed and shook his head. "Hope? Hope, baby, there is no one here but us."

"What?" She stomped into the living room. "Why are you mocking me?"

"Because that's what you wanted to hear. Why would you care if someone was here anyway? You don't know if you want me so why not give someone else a chance?"

"Now why would you say that?"

"You are desperately searching for a reason, any reason, to leave me. A content person wouldn't do that."

"That is not true"

"Are you sure about that?"

"Do I look sure of anything?" Hope stood with her head in her hands. She massaged her temples.

"I ask again; what do you want from me?"

"I want to know you really want me."

"I do, baby. Do you think I would've asked you to marry me if I didn't?"

The doorbell rang.

Hope took the opportunity to escape. She looked out the window to find an Asian woman at the door. She talked over her shoulder. "Honey, did you order Chinese food?"

"No, I didn't. Why?"

Hope opened the door. "May I help you?"

"I need to see Richard."

"Who are you?"

"I'm his girl, Mi Ling."

"My who?" Hope stepped back and then turned to Richard. "You know what? I don't have time for this. This is why I am the way I am, Richard. You don't know what you want, so I'll make the decision for you. I'm gone and here's your ring." She threw the stunning ring in Mi Ling's face and then pushed past her.

Hope yelled at herself all the way home. As she walked into her dorm room the phone rang.

"Hello, Hope?"

"Mica?"

"Did I catch you at a bad time?"

"Are you kidding? Your timing couldn't be more perfect."

"Are you okay?"

"I'm fine. Why?"

"You sound like you've been crying."

"I can't believe you still know me like that."

"Of course I do. You're my soul mate."

"Then why haven't we spoken before now?"

"I've been seeing other people; you've been seeing other people. That's the down side of long-distance relationships."

"Wait. How did you know? You've been calling?"

"Of course I have."

"And you talked to Nicole?"

"Yes, but I'm not angry. I dated Trina from your flight so if you can accept that, I can accept whatever you've done."

"Trina? Of all people. She knew how I felt about you. How could she?"

"Hope, let's be realistic. You accepted a marriage proposal. I just dated the girl. In fact we only went out twice."

"Were you two intimate?"

"Come on, you know me better than that. Of course not."

"Why not? Did God convict you?"

"That and the fact she wasn't you."

"So what exactly did Nicole tell you about my relationship with Richard?"

"I know everything."

"Nicole needs to mind her own business and keep her big mouth shut."

"Stop, you know that's your girl. She was just worried about you and felt I could help."

"Is there anything she hasn't told you?"

"Does it matter? Let's just pick up where we left off. We're going to be together soon."

"Are you serious?"

"Yes, I'm serious. Do you think you still want to be with me?"

"Yes, I know I do."

"Then let's do this. I know you were reclassified, so when you get to Wichita Falls we'll hook up."

"I have a mess to clean up here. Are you sure you aren't upset with me?"

"Are you pregnant?"

"No."

"Married?"

"Not yet."

"Then there's nothing to be upset about. Let it go girl. It's all good."

"But I have to work with this man for three more weeks."

"I trust you."

"You're crazy to trust so blindly, but I love you for it."

"I love you, too. See ya soon."

Hope wanted to strangle Nicole, but seeing as how her espionage facilitated Mica's return, she let her live.

Hope used a week of sick leave to stave a confrontation with Richard. The third day into her absence, he called. From the rising of the sun to the going down of the same, he left pathetic messages on her answering machine. On day five, longing for answers, Hope picked up the phone.

"Were you going to tell me you were leaving in two weeks?"

"Is that all you have to say to me?"

"We need to talk. It's not what it looked like."

"I didn't hear you trying to explain anything in front of

ya girl."

"She is not my girl; she is an ex-girlfriend."

"Uh-huh or maybe she was Ms. San Antonio."

"No, I really did have my daughter. Call my ex-wife if you don't believe me."

"You've got me messed up. I don't have time for your ex-factors."

"Can we just meet somewhere?"

"What's the point?"

"So we can talk."

"We're talking now."

"You know what I mean."

"Why are you even bothering to mend this? Some things can't be fixed; perhaps this is one of them. You're leaving for Kunsan and I'm leaving for Sheppard. Let's just cut our losses and quit now."

"Do you really believe I'm ahead? I am miserable without you. Do you want to call it quits or are you sulking like a spoiled brat?"

"I don't know what I want anymore. I wanted you to be different. I wanted you to really care about me. I wanted you to fall so deeply in love with me; you'd rather die than hurt me."

"I deserved that."

"Get out of my life, Richard." She paused, You deserved that too."

"Hold up. Last time I checked you still had a boyfriend. What was his name, Michael?"

"His name is Mica and you knew that when you proposed to me. Apparently we're still together. He called earlier tonight, knows all about you and still wants me. So there!"

"I'm sure he does, but who do you want?"

"Mighty confident aren't we?"

"Not really. I just want to know who you want."

"I didn't want you to cheat on me with Mi Ling."

"I did not cheat on you with her and even if I would have, you still have Mica?"

"I told you about him from day one. I can't believe…forget it. I can't even talk to you right now. Are we ever going to stop fighting?"

"We're fighting because we're frustrated. Don't talk. I'm coming over."

"No, I don't want you to come over. If we fight in person we'll end up in bed."

"Well let's stop all this nonsense and get to the good part."

"Didn't you get the good part from Mi Ling? It's barely been a week and you're tired of her already?"

"Quit playing. I told you there is nothing going on between me and Mi Ling."

"Well maybe you should tell her that."

"I'm tired of arguing. How about you come over here?"

"Now you want me to come over there? You have really lost your mind."

"I see this is not going anywhere so please take note. I know you love me and you know I love you; so when you're ready I will be waiting. Just hurry, baby. You're leaving in two weeks."

"Wait! Why did she come over, Richard? What exactly did Mi Ling want if it wasn't you?"

"She wanted to cause drama and judging by your reaction, her mission was accomplished."

"So she's been harassing you?"

"Yes, I guess you could say that."

"And you didn't tell me because?"

"I didn't think you'd understand."

"Then you were right because I don't. Is that all you have to say in your defense?"

"Hope, I still want to marry you despite the fact you threw my ring."

"Do you honestly think I could trust you in a long-distance relationship, when you can't be faithful with me in the same city?"

"Baby, just give me one more chance. It looks bad but I'm an innocent man."

"Why should I? Just because you have 'Big Poppa' on your license plates does not make you Biggie! You didn't deserve the chance you got."

"Fine, I'm on my way over. I guarantee you can't tell me face to face."

"You'll be wasting your time. I have nothing left to say to you."

Twenty minutes passed and Richard pulled up outside of Hope's dorm. He honked like a gaggle of geese flying in v-formation. Embarrassed, she ran downstairs.

He flung open the car door. "I figured you'd see things my way if I came over and acted like a fool."

"Whatever. You better be happy I care what people think, otherwise I'd leave your stupid butt out here."

She got into his car and he drove away.

"Hope, I don't want you to go."

"Why are you doing this?"

"Doing what? Begging you to stay with me?"

"Yes...why? More airmen will be arriving soon and

I'm sure one of them would be more than happy to take my place."

"You know I've never dated an airman before you. Furthermore, you know you don't want to leave me."

"I know you're a jerk."

"I know I'm still in love with you."

"You have five minutes to explain yourself," she folded her arms across her chest. "Talk."

"I know I messed up."

"Keep going…"

"I'm sorry."

"Four and a half minutes."

"Let's drive to the airfield. Do I have your permission to do that?"

"Since when did you need my permission to do anything?"

Richard drove to the airfield they used to frequent for a relaxing night of star gazing. Hope hoped that the nostalgia would cause her to remember why she loved him so much.

Richard turned on the stereo and played a mixed tape created for her. "Why are you so bitter? You know I haven't been with Mi Ling since I've been seeing you. So what's your real problem?"

"In a word—betrayed. How did you think I'd feel when she rolled up to your spot, my spot, like it was nothing? Not to mention the fact that I'd dropped in by surprise. How do I know that you didn't call her over or that she doesn't stop over on a regular?"

"How do I know you're not planning to be with Mica?"

"You can't compare Mica to Mi Ling. First of all, you

knew about him from the beginning. I can't say the same about Mi Ling. I opened up to you about my past and allowed you into my heart. And what did you do with that power? You used my vulnerability against me. I hate you!"

"No, you don't hate anyone. Don't say that!"

"I really do hate you."

"It's not in your nature. Are we going to get past this?"

"Give me one reason why we should?"

"I love you!"

"That may have worked before but not anymore. You don't know the meaning of the word."

"I'm going to pray to God on your behalf."

"You do that and while you're talking to God, ask Him what He thinks about us having sex."

"Did that make you feel better?"

"Actually yes... it did."

"I thought we were getting married."

"That doesn't change the Word. The Bible doesn't say have sex, if you think you're going to get married. It's better to marry than to burn which implies until you are married, sex is a sin. Now change the subject. You're really making me mad. Better yet, take me back to my dorm."

"Kiss me first."

"I don't even like you right now. Kiss you? Not!"

"Kiss me to prove that you dislike me. If you don't feel anything from the kiss, I will take you back to your dorm; no questions asked."

"That has to be the dumbest thing I've ever heard you say." She leaned over and kissed him.

Forty minutes later, as they dressed and wiped the

footprints from the windows, guilt returned to Hope. Richard tried to justify their romp by classifying it as an act of love.

"God is love, right? So what's the big deal?"

Hope bit her lip and stared out the window.

~~~~~~~~

The days passed quickly and before Hope knew it, she was at the departure gate waiting to board her flight to Sheppard Air Force Base.

Richard rubbed the back of her hand. "Call me as soon as you arrive on base. I should be out to visit you in a few weeks."

Tears formed in Hope's eyes. "This is harder than I expected."

"You'll be all right. I love you."

"I love you, too."

Richard presented the ring that Hope had thrown at Mi Ling and placed it back on her finger.

Hope cried even harder.

"Stop crying, baby. People are looking at you."

"I don't care about these people. Let them look. I don't want to go."

"Yes, you do. This was your decision, remember? We're gonna make it. So go before you miss your flight. Everything will be fine."

Hope got on the plane. She loved Richard more than she thought. But Mica was still coming to Sheppard and she believed that she loved him too. Then again, Hope loved everybody. She fell quickly trying to plug a void that could only be filled with God's unconditional love.
~~~~~~~~

Chapter Eleven

Rafael

Hope's reclassification from intelligence to medical transferred her to Wichita Falls, Texas as a mental health assistant. Although she was tired of Richard's deceitfulness, she longed to talk with him. The call never came.

In medical class, Hope daydreamed and doodled on her notebook. Oftentimes she wrote Richard's name with swirls and hearts all around it. She even assessed a value to their love using the letters in their names.

"What's that you got there, Picasso?" a handsome classmate asked.

Hope slammed shut her notebook. "Oh, nothing."

"Didn't look like nothing."

"Before you go any further with this small talk, I've got a boyfriend and a fiancé.

The confusion that rolled onto his Latino face screamed for clarification. Hope delivered a lengthy soliloquy about her two men.

"Oh, hi, I'm Hope."

He shook his head. "I'm Rafael."

"So you think I'm pretty crazy, huh?'

"Yeah you are pretty and crazy too. It's ironic that you'll be working in the psychiatric department at the hospital."

"Excuse me?"

"Nothing."

"Well you have a good day." Hope turned to walk away. "I'll see on Monday."

"You, too. Hey wait." Rafael jogged to catch up with her. "What are you doing tonight?"

"Going to the mall and calling Richard as usual. Why?"

"I was wondering if maybe you'd like to rent a movie and hang out with me."

"What do you mean? We hang out everyday in class?"

"I know but I mean hang outside of class."

"Weren't you listening to the story I just told? I already have a fiancé and a boyfriend. Why on earth would you want to get involved with me, too?"

"Who said anything about getting involved? I just want to hang out."

Hope smiled as she took time to look at the fine specimen of a man who stood before her. Rafael was younger than her by four or five years. As a Mexican American, he had a strong Spanish accent which Hope found sexy.

"Has anyone ever told you that you look li---"

"Jay Hernandez, the actor."

"Yeah."

"All the time. I take it as a compliment. Thanks."

"So what movie did you want to see?"

"I really want to see *I Like It Like That,* but if you want to see something else that'd be fine."

Hope smiled wide. "That is one of my favorite movies."

"So you've seen it already?"

"Yes, but I can see it again. I love that movie."

"Then it's a date." A sheepish grin appeared on Rafael's face.

Hope bit her lip. "A date?"

"It'll be fun hanging out with you." He smiled wider as he started to walk away and then he turned back around. "Where should we meet? And what time would be good for you?"

"How about at the picnic tables by our dorm at seven?"

"Sounds good to me. See you then."

By five o'clock, Hope became reluctant to follow through with "hanging out." She had committed to focusing her attention to self-development and a deeper relationship with God. She realized that she needed unconditional love to fill the abyss in her soul, yet she sought the affection of men and landed in a love triangle.

To ease her conscience, she called Richard again. The weekend ritual left her empty and Richard's voicemail full. She speculated that he ignored her calls because he was seeing someone else or maybe he was busy with work. When she ended the third message, she decided to check her mail.

She walked to the post office a few blocks away. She opened her mailbox and several letters tumbled out of it. She received a letter from her dad, a letter from her aunt and a letter from Richard.

Hey baby what's up? Let me start by saying I miss you so much!

"Humph, that's hard to believe."

How are you adjusting to your new base? I heard they assigned you to the dorms by accident. It's not so bad. I hope you get everything straightened out soon. The last thing I need is to have one of those young bucks hitting on my baby girl.

"Too late."

Anyway, I'm headed to Phoenix this weekend with my boys. I'll be thinking about you the entire trip. I miss hearing your sweet, alluring voice. Give me a call and please make it soon.

"Like you're gonna pick up the phone."

P.S. Attached are some pictures of your man to remind you exactly how handsome I am.

Hope tore through the envelope. She ripped the corner of the picture of Richard, adorned in his dress blues with the American flag next to him. Hope loved to see her men in uniform. In the next picture, Richard stood on the west perimeter of the airfield with his right foot staged on a large rock. The last picture showed Richard seated on his living-room couch with a full smile and blushed cheeks.

"He never smiles, unless…" Hope looked a little closer at the photo. She saw a reflection in the mirror mounted on the wall behind Richard. She couldn't make out the image with 100% accuracy. She called Richard expecting to get his voicemail.

"Hello?"

"Hey, Richard. How are you?"

"Great now that I'm talking to you! Did you get my pictures? Baby, I miss you so much."

"Yeah I got them." She paused to count to three. "Look, about the pictures…"

"Your man looks good, doesn't he?"

"Are you still my man?"

"Here we go again. Don't start, baby."

"Don't start? Let's see, you haven't called me since I arrived here."

"That's not true. I left a lot of messages but based on your comment, you never received them, huh?"

"No, I did not!"

"I don't know why. I've been calling."

"Whatever, Richard. Have you been seeing Mi Ling?"

"No, no baby. Why would you ask that?"

"Well, you're smiling in this picture in your living room."

"And…"

"And who took the picture?"

"I took the picture with my tripod."

"You took the picture recently?"

"Yes, why?"

"Because you always try to look hard in pictures unless..."

"Unless what?"

"Unless a woman is making you blush and you don't realize that you're smiling."

"That's crazy. So you think some woman took the picture? What woman would be in my living room?"

"That's what I would like to know. Don't lie."

"Again, I don't know where all of this is coming from? I tell you I miss you, send pictures and you accuse me of cheating. You better stop watching those soap operas because they are messing with your mind." Richard laughed.

"I am serious! Why are you laughing? I'm going to ask you one more time. If you did something man up and confess because if you tell me that you didn't, and I find out you did, it's over!"

"For the last time, the only woman in my living room was my tripod, Ms. Lady. Quit tripping!"

"Uh-huh, so where are you?"

"I'm getting ready to leave for Phoenix. I'll be there until next Sunday."

"I thought you were coming to see me before your trip to Phoenix."

"I was but you know, things just happened."

"No, I don't know. And I don't want to hear any shady explanations either."

"What is that supposed to mean?"

"I have to go."

"I love you, Hope."

"Have fun in Phoenix."

She ended the call, ran to the photo lab down the street. As she approached Wal-Mart, she saw Rafael leaving the florist with a bouquet of assorted flowers. She ducked behind a vending machine.

"I had a feeling he was going to treat our evening like a date."

She watched him walk to his car and then she sprinted inside the store. The technician promised to enlarge the photo in a few minutes. Hope waited at the counter. She tried to occupy herself with the camera accessories, but anxiety got the best of her. Her heart beat faster and faster. She broke out into sweat. She said a quick prayer for Richard's safety.

Fifteen minutes into eternity, the technician handed Hope a poster-size envelope. Careful not to rip the photo, she removed it. Her mouth gaped open. Just as she suspected; Mi Ling was the reflection in the mirror. The flash from the camera blocked part of her face, but her petite body was visible. She wore a red, satin kimono-style bathrobe with a large yellow dragon. Chinese symbols encircled the winding beast. She took a deep breath, gathered her belongings, headed back toward the dorm. She still needed to get ready to hang out with Rafael.

During her fast-paced walk, Hope contemplated disclosing the evidence to Richard. She decided to let it fester to give her time to develop a retaliation plan. When she arrived at the dorm, the front-desk receptionist gave her a telegram. Mica wanted her to call as soon as possible. Frustrated and already behind schedule, she called.

"Hello, Mica, it's Hope."

"Hey, girl, what's up? So I take it you received my message?"

"Yes. How are things going with your base transfer?"

"Great I guess. But I might have to go to Abilene, Texas instead of Wichita Falls. I won't know for a few weeks. Either way we'll be together, right?"

"Of course, honey. Abilene is only a few hours away. Besides it's still closer than where you're stationed now."

"So what's been up with you? Are you still dealing with that Richard guy?"

"No. He's officially a part of my past."

"Then I guess that makes me your future and there isn't anyone else I'd rather spend my life with."

"I can't wait to see you, Mica. How soon do you think it'll be?"

"Who knows? It gives me something to look forward to."

"That's sweet. Honey, I gotta go."

"Don't give my love away."

"Wouldn't think of it."

"Go out and have fun, but not too much. Remember I love you. New York in the house! Girl, represent."

"You are so crazy!"

"That's why you love me so much."

Hope was more confused than ever. What had she done to deserve his love? Was he compelled to love her and only her? Unworthy. She knew she had issues but he knew she had them too. Her defense mechanism compelled her to chase men away before they had the option to leave. Yet, Mica wanted to stay. What made him so different?

She hurried to her room for a quick shower. She wore a short mini skirt and a cute top to show off all of her curvy assets. No virtuous woman here. She met up with Rafael and they walked to the Base Exchange; a one-stop shopping center for military personnel. They rented the movie, returned to the dorm.

During a vivid sex scene, Rafael turned to Hope. "If you married me, what do you think our kids would look like?"

"You said this wasn't a date and you've got us married with kids."

He laughed. "I'm just kidding. Don't act like you didn't notice that the main character was Black and her husband was Puerto Rican."

"I noticed, but you're Mexican not Puerto Rican, right?"

"Yeah but I'm talking about the cultural differences in raising biracial and bilingual kids."

"Oh, well that's a little deep for our first night out, don't you think?"

"I guess you're right. So on a lighter note; what do you want to be when you grow up?"

"What?"

"You're thinking too hard. Answer the question."

"Happy! What about you?"

"I want to be happy, too! See how much we have in common?"

"I'm hungry. What about you?"

"Do you like pizza?"

"My favorite."

They paused the video, walked to the neighborhood pizza parlor. While they waited on their to-go pizza, Hope bumped into her friend, Amanda. Amanda knew Rafael from class so an introduction was not needed.

"Hello, Hope, Rafael. I'm so happy I ran into you guys. Arnold and I are getting married in three weeks. I know that it's short notice, but Hope would you be my maid of honor?"

"Sure, I'd be honored."

"Not so fast, there's a slight catch."

"Okay and it is…?"

"The wedding is in Abilene, Texas."

"I don't see the catch."

"We would have to pick up Arnold from Goodfellow. I know Richard is still stationed there so would that be a problem?

"No, actually I need the closure."

"Are you sure you're ready to move on, Hope? Don't do it on my behalf."

"Amanda, trust me, I'll be fine."

"Great. Then I'll see you both in Abilene."

Rafael paid for the pizza. They sat at a table to eat and chat.

"So are you going to be okay with breaking off your engagement?"

"Are you kidding? The jerk cheated on me. Of course."

"Are you sure?"

"Yes, he sent pictures today to prove it."

"Why would anyone send self-incriminating pictures?"

"Plain stupidity but that's what I get for trusting him."

"Did he offer an explanation?"

"He offered his feeble attempt of the truth."

"What did he say?"

"He said he took the picture with his tripod but I knew better so I had the picture enlarged to analyze it. The flash in the reflection distorted the image but it was obliviously the woman he used to date."

"You went through all of that trouble to find out if he was cheating on you? Are you sure you're over him?"

"I don't ever recall saying that I was over him. I know I can't marry him, so the engagement is definitely off. I warned you before you asked me to hang out that my love life was a hot mess."

"I know you did but like I told you; I just want your friendship." Rafael drummed his fingers across the pizza box. "Well…"

"Well what?"

"I lied." He leaned over the table, kissed her.

"Where did that come from?"

"It came from my heart."

She wrinkled her forehead, cocked her upper lip.

"I've wanted to kiss you ever since you entered my

class."

"Really and you didn't because?"

"Because you wouldn't stop talking about Richard and Mica."

"Okay but I'm still talking about them so what's changed?"

"Richard cheated on you, so you'll be ending things soon."

"That still leaves Mica."

"Mica was never the competition. Richard had your heart."

"You really think so?"

"He had some kind of hold on you."

"Why do you say that?"

"Amanda's fiancé, Arnold, was stationed with you at Goodfellow, right?"

"Yeah, but I vaguely remember him."

"Well, Arnold told Amanda that Richard was cheating on you with another student."

"I asked Richard about that and he said that Arnold was upset because he was fazed back for underage drinking. He got charged for a crime and lied in retaliation."

"He got an Article 15?" Rafael wiped table crumbs onto a napkin, crumpled the napkin, tossed it on his plate.

"Yes, Amanda said that he did. So I believed Richard and dismissed Arnold's accusation."

"Perhaps there was more to the story."

"Maybe, but if you knew this before, why did you listen to my delusional version of my relationship with Richard?"

"It gave me an excuse to spend some time with you."

"But had you told me sooner you could've spent even more time."

"Not likely. You wouldn't have believed me and possibly hated me for being the bearer of bad news. I never would've stood a chance."

"You're probably right. What makes you think you have a chance now?"

"You kissed me back."

"Maybe I just like to kiss. That doesn't make you special." She flashed a huge smile.

"Do you think we can *hang out* more often?"

"Define *hang out* because to my understanding friends hang out."

"Okay, we're friends."

"But friends don't kiss each other on the mouth with tongue!"

"Okay, then we're no longer friends."

Hope stood. "Walk me back to the dorm. It's getting late and I have youth group in the morning."

"Youth group with Sergeant Sanders?"

"Don't perpetrate like you go."

"I know but Sergeant Sanders asked me to go just yesterday, I promise."

"Do you go to church?"

"Yes, the chapel on base."

"Which service?"

"Usually the 0900 gospel service."

"No way, I attend the 1100 gospel service. Maybe we can start going together."

"Sounds good to me."

"So are you coming to young-adult group tomorrow morning?"

"Yes, I think I will."

"Great I'll see you there." They arrived at the dorm lobby.

"I'd walk you to your room but you know the rules: no males allowed."

"No problem."

"Well can I kiss you good night?"

"You want to kiss me right here? Public displays of affection are prohibited, remember? No PDA; check your manual."

Rafael smiled, grabbed Hope by the waist.

"Then perhaps we should pay a little visit to PDA park."

PDA Park was named by the airmen as a place to make-out in public. No authority figures enforced the rules as long as the affection remained in the park.

"That's not gonna happen."

"But I've wanted you forever."

"Forever is a long time so your wait will seem like nothing." She pried his hands off her waist, gave him a hug and a quick peck on the cheek. "I'll see you at young-adult group."

He waited a moment as Hope left for her room. She wanted to get hot and bothered with Rafael. She was desperate for affection, but knew he was not the answer. She returned to her room alone, but with great peace and a little pride.

The next morning, the alarm chimed. Hope slapped the snooze a time or two. By the time she finally awoke, she was almost late to the group meeting.

"Good morning, Airman Tolliver."

"Good morning, Sergeant Sanders. I thought I was late," she looked around the meeting room, "but where is our guest speaker?"

"You are late. He's already setup and waiting at the podium." Sergeant Sanders leaned back in his padded chair pointing toward the speaker.

Embarrassed, Hope scurried to a seat. She shimmied in the metal fold-out chair to warm it, noticed the speaker was watching. She nodded to indicate that she was ready.

The guest speaker said, "Good morning, ladies and gentlemen. My name is LaMarr Wilson and I work for the nonprofit organization Ocir Philanthropy. We conduct a mentor program that helps individuals understand the Lord's calling on their lives. Before I begin my presentation, I would like for each of you to introduce yourselves. Who would like to start?"

A strong, confident voice projected from across the room. "I'll start. My name is Hope Tolliver."

"I'm Sergeant Sanders."

"Philip Cartwright."

"Nona Edwards."

LaMarr Wilson acknowledged each attendee with a nod and a smile.

"Rafael Rodriguez."

"Michael Bollinger."

"Adrian Concepcion."

"Thank you, class. Let's begin, shall we? "

From the front of the room, a young man with a prideful countenance said, "Yes, sir. We shall." A grin emerged.

Ignoring the smug antics, LaMarr continued. "I am here to share information on a topic few care to discuss.

Did you know the number one killer among the human race today is abortion?

Silence bounced off the cinderblock walls and ricocheted onto the vinyl floor. The bellow of a lieutenant conducting exercises on the drill line echoed through the windows.

"Hut-two-three-four! Pick your feet up cadets! Precise movement demonstrates your strength! Pick those feet up!"

Can anyone tell me who Margaret Sanger is?" LaMarr coughed to regain the group's attention. "Hope, since you started the introductions, perhaps you could enlighten the group. Who is Margaret Sanger?"

Hope flashed LaMarr a smile, pressed the wrinkles out of her jeans with her hands. "I don't know."

LaMarr said, "Margaret Sanger spawned the International Planned Parenthood Federation. She was a proponent of forced eugenics, segregation, abortion, birth control and sexual immorality."

Phillip raised his hand.

"Yes, Phillip"

"What does she have to do with anything?"

"Excellent question. She also founded Planned Parenthood. She stated that one purpose for creating this organization was so abortion could destroy the Black race."

Hope gasped, slumped in her seat.

"Here are a few of her quotes: 'Birth control must lead ultimately to a cleaner race.'" He paused, looked at the class. "'We should hire three or four colored ministers, preferably with social-service backgrounds and with engaging personalities. The most successful educational approach to the Negro is through a religious appeal.'"

Disgust, shock, disbelief permeated the now attentive group.

"'Eugenic sterilization is an urgent need. We must prevent multiplication of this bad stock.' Sixty-five percent of abortion clinics are in low-income, minority communities and that is not by coincidence."

With a subtle quiver in her voice, Nona said, "Abortion is a matter of choice. I don't see anything wrong with it. If I couldn't take care of my child I wouldn't want it to suffer in this world."

LaMarr narrowed his eyes, hardened his voice, leaned forward. "Nona, your attitude is shared by thousands of young ladies which has resulted in an increase in abortions. Unfortunately women would rather kill their child then allow someone else to take care of it. Loving families who are unable to conceive wait years to adopt. The adoption agencies are suffering while the abortion clinics flourish." He leaned back, softened his voice. "Your baby could be the next Einstein, president or even international evangelist. Every time a child is born, God gets the Glory. He's Creator. Sadly enough, Margaret Sanger's tactics are working."

Michael Bollinger, the six-foot-six grizzly bear of the class, said "I had no idea. What can we do to stop it?"

"Open your mouth and spread the word. Write to the government." LaMarr stared out at the group. "You can make a difference. Abortion is appalling and it was created to kill and destroy. We have to fight for the abundant life of God's babies."

Nona smiled. "I want to help put a stop to abortion."

The group erupted into a series of side conversations.

LaMarr interrupted. "Does anyone have a question or anything they'd like to share about abortion?"

Adrian, who had been quiet throughout the session, now spoke. "I do."

"Yes, Adrian."

His eyes watered.

"Are you okay?"

"Yes, it's just that my girl…um…yesterday my girl had an abortion." Large tears dropped from his eyes and splattered onto the table.

Hope's heart poured out for him yet she sat speechless. She had no idea what to say to console him or articulate her condolences.

Rafael placed his hands on the table, leveraged himself, stood. "Man, I can't even imagine how it would feel to lose a child but I know what it's like to lose a parent. My dad died less than a year ago. I'm still mourning his death." With calculated steps, he walked toward Adrian. "People told me it would get better with time but I can't tell. I still trust that God will see me through and I know He will. He promised that He'd never leave me nor forsake me and that's real." He gave Adrian a man hug, spoke in his ear, returned to his seat.

LaMarr intervened. "Both of you have endured rough circumstances but God said that we will endure trials and tribulations until He returns. I'll be praying for you guys."

Nona asked Adrian, "Does your girlfriend know the Lord?"

Michael said, "If she knew the Lord, don't you think she would've kept her legs closed?"

Nona rolled her eyes. "Augh, Michael that was awful. Unless you've never committed a sin in your perfect, limited life, refrain from judging others."

"Give me a break, Nona. You're only defending her because sluts have to stick together."

LaMarr interjected. "Enough, Michael! This is an emotional topic and for some it's personal so I ask that you be considerate before blurting out cruel, insensitive or offensive statements."

Michael said, "Why do we have to walk on eggshells? I wanna know if Hope's ever had an abortion?"

Rafael said, "I don't know you, man but you're way out of line."

"No, it's okay Rafael. I'll answer him." Hope turned to the grizzly. "No, Michael, I have never had an abortion, but I have had a miscarriage. Are you going to judge me for that?"

"No, a miscarriage is way different than an abortion."

"True, but my miscarriage was the product of fornication. So are you saying that one sin is worse than the other?"

Adamant to defend her honor, Rafael said, "It's none of his business, Hope. Don't even entertain him with an explanation."

"I appreciate your concern, Rafael, but it's okay. I was diagnosed at the age of fourteen with endometriosis." Reading the ignorance on her peers' faces, she continued, "Endometriosis is not an STD. It's a condition that developed prior to sexual activity. It used to be called the Career Woman's Disease because it afflicted women in their late thirties who had never had children. The disease makes it difficult to conceive and carry a child to term. In other words, they could miscarry like I did."

Michael said, "I'm sorry, Hope."

"It's okay. There's not a day that goes by that I don't think about my baby. So, please be careful how you come at people. Try not to judge or make premature assumptions."

LaMarr said, "If you want to do anything, pray for people. Show them the love of God. There's no condemnation in Christ. Lead them to Christ and He can do the convicting instead of you driving them away by condemning. Adrian, how's your girlfriend doing now?"

"Who cares about her? Our baby is dead!"

Hope cleared her throat, said, "I'm sorry, Adrian. I don't know what else to say."

"Because there is nothing left to say. What type of person is that selfish?"

"Me, I guess."

"What? You said you never had an abortion."

"I didn't, I had a miscarriage. I never told anyone until today."

"Not even the baby's father? That doesn't even sound like you."

"It doesn't sound like me now but it was definitely me then. I was afraid and I didn't want him to stay with me out of obligation. I'd like to believe I would have told him at some point during the pregnancy but I didn't get far enough to know for sure."

"Are you ever going to tell him? I still think he has a right to know."

"I agree. Hopefully I'll have the strength to tell him one day."

"You are stronger than you think, Hope."

"I pray you're right."

Adrian gazed attentively into Hope's eyes. She laid her head on his chest and cried. He consoled her for the remainder of group.

"I'm sorry, but I have to go now. If you have any additional questions or concerns, my number is on my card." He shuffled a handful cards and dealt them around the table.

The group applauded.

Adrian said, "Hope is amazing! Never take her for granted and treat her well. If I'd done that, maybe my girl wouldn't have had an abortion." He used the tips of his fingers to lift Hope's chin. "Tell your baby's daddy. It's the right thing to do." He kissed her forehead, stood. "I better get back to the dorm. See you guys later."

Rafael nodded. "Bye, Adrian. Give me a call if you need me, bro." Rafael turned to Hope, shook his head.

"What are you shaking your head at me for?"

"Your life is plagued with drama. I go out on one date with you and I've gone through an emotional roller coaster so intense I feel like I just returned from war."

"Oh and it's my fault?" she sucked her teeth.

"No, it's not your fault at all. Even if it were you'd be worth it."

"You don't know me very well."

They left for the mall and then to the movies. Afterwards, they drove out to the country and looked at the stars from the back of Rafael's pick-up truck. Hope lay in Rafael's arms as he opened up about his father. They talked throughout the night about God, death and sin. He believed that Hope was his soul mate. He described vivid dreams about his father giving his approval of their relationship.

Rafael had a demented relationship with God. He believed that making love was a deep spiritual connection to God even if it was out of covenant.

Hope didn't agree with his perspective but she willingly transferred spirits to create yet another soul tie. Parked on the side of the road, in the back of his truck, they engaged in one of countless practices of fornication. The dating rhythm was predictable: started with discussion about his father, then love and finally destiny. By the end of the conversation, they'd go at it like savage beasts only to long for the next entanglement. The ritual occurred almost daily and on occasion several times a day.

Rafael and Hope embarked on a strange routine of sex, church, sex, church, church and more sex. They grew negligent with their excursions to the point of a potential arrest for indecent exposure. They were under the bleachers on base in broad daylight.

All rationale had escaped them. Hope couldn't think sensibly in his presence. Who would've suspected an initially low-profile friend would cause such a ruckus?

Chapter Twelve

Ryan

Hope and Rafael worked well together. They partnered on church-related events for the youth, they studied for medical exams, they gazed at the stars and enjoyed frequent fiestas. She had all but forgotten about the men of her past, until she received a call from Ryan.

"Hope?"

"Yes," she paused to put a name to the voice. "Ryan, is that you?"

"Yeah, look I'm in Texas on business and I was wondering if you were available for lunch?"

"What? Today?"

"I know I should've given you more notice. Can I be honest with you?"

"Sure. I expect nothing less."

"This isn't the first time I've been in town. It's just the first time I've mustered up enough nerve to contact you."

"You mean you've kept track of my whereabouts all of this time?"

"Yes, through an intense tracking system called Sarah."

"Mommy gave you my number?"

"Yep, so I guess she likes me after all." He chuckled. "Anyway, are you busy around one?"

"Yes."

"Maybe next time. Your mom told me that you were doing it big with your new career and all, but I just never fathomed you'd be too busy to make moves with me."

"Yes, I'd love to see you. Not yes, I'm too busy. Where would you like to meet?"

"I'll be on base but we can meet in the city if you'd like."

"Works for me. I'm seeing this guy and I'd rather not have to explain you to him."

"I understand. How about Buenos downtown?"

"Buenos at one. I'll see you there."

Hope hung up the phone just as guilt settled on her shoulders. She wanted to tell Rafael that she needed to see Ryan to come clean about the baby, but would that justify the meeting? How about a case of selective amnesia? The latter would have to suffice. So reminiscent of college, Hope escaped for a secret rendezvous with Ryan.

Hope arrived before Ryan. The host informed her that a table had been reserved for the Spencer party. Impressed, she was seated. She tapped her foot and twirled her hair.

Ryan walked toward her. His commanding gait made several women take notice. He had on jeans and a designer sports shirt but his presence made him look like royalty.

Hope sat erect in the seat. She exhaled with her lower lip extended to air dry the sweat that beaded on her forehead.

"Hey, beautiful. How are you?" He greeted Hope with a soft kiss on the cheek.

"I'm fine."

"Yes, you still are."

"So what's been up with you, Ryan? Are you still breaking hearts?"

"Whatever. If memory serves me correctly you broke my heart. But never mind that, girl, you really look nice."

"Thank you, so do you. I think I know you pretty well so what's really going on?"

"What do you mean?"

"It took a lot for you to call Mommy, so what's behind this engagement?"

"Are you implying I have a hidden agenda?"

"No, I'm not implying; I know you do, so don't play."

"Are you seeing anybody, Hope?"

"Yes, as a matter of fact I am. Are you?"

"Yes, I'm seeing a teacher who reminds me of you."

"Is that good or bad?"

"You tell me."

"I don't know. But before we go any further I have something to tell you."

"Okay… I'm listening."

"Well, remember when we broke up?"

"Of course I do. It was an incident uneasy to forget."

"Well I wasn't completely honest about the reason I walked away."

"I'm still listening."

"I was pregnant."

"I knew it! I knew it! But my heart wouldn't permit me to believe you'd keep something like that from me. In fact you specifically told me you weren't. Well, what did we have?"

"We," she hesitated, expelled a sad sigh, "had a miscarriage. Did you think I'd conceal a kid all of these years?"

"You never know. After all you did lie about being pregnant."

"I deserved that. I'm so sorry."

"What are you sorry about?"

"I wanted to tell you that I was pregnant but I just couldn't tolerate your reaction. When I had finally garnered the nerve to tell you, I miscarried."

"You still should've told me."

"I know, but I was so miserable. I thought it would be easier to keep it to myself."

"So what prompted you to confess now after all of this time?"

"A dear friend showed me the error of my ways. He made me realize how selfish I was for hiding this from you."

"You weren't selfish; perplexed maybe."

"No, he was right."

"I still can't believe this. If you would have told me about the pregnancy sooner, I could've taken better care of you and maybe you wouldn't have miscarried."

"And that is exactly why I didn't want to tell you. I knew you'd try to take responsibility but there was nothing anyone could have done."

"You don't know that."

"True, but I have endometriosis. Who knows if I'll ever carry a baby to term. I felt inadequate as your woman, lover and even as a friend."

"You were more than adequate in our relationship. A part of me wants to be upset with you, but my heart refuses to let me. Tell me why I'm still in love with you after all of this time."

"I can't answer that for you. Are you sure it's me you love?"

"I never stopped loving you, Hope. I can't imagine what you went through... alone at that. Not to be morbid or anything, but how many months were you?"

"Three."

"You never cease to amaze me. Oh the tangled web we weave..."

"I cannot apologize enough."

"It's water under the bridge. We can't change the past so let it go. I'm not hungry anymore. Do you mind if we get out of here?" Ryan dropped a ten-dollar bill on the table.

"Not at all. Lead the way."

Ryan helped Hope out of the chair, led her to his hotel. A tinge of fear taunted her when they entered the lobby, but she followed him to his room anyway. Once inside, Ryan tossed his keys on the nightstand and sat on the bed. Hope sat on a sofa located on the other side of the room.

"Why are you sitting so far away?"

"No reason."

"Then come closer. I won't bite...I promise." He laughed.

"What is so funny?"

"Nothing. I still can't believe you were my baby's mama."

"That's not funny."

"It isn't but I couldn't resist."

She tried to stifle the waterfall, but tears cascaded down her face.

"Aw, Hope. I didn't mean to make you cry." Ryan walked to the sofa, took Hope by the hand, helped her stand. He let his hand rest on her waist as he moved to stand behind her. He lifted her hair, gently kissed her neck.

"Ryan, what do you think you're doing?"

"Shhhh quiet. Just kiss me."

Captivated, Hope turned to face Ryan. Memories of their past encounters flooded her. She wanted to resist, walk away, but instead she kissed him. When he caressed her, she panicked.

"Ryan, I don't think this is a good idea."

He placed his index finger on her lips, kissed her as he moved her toward the bed. At the edge of the bed, he undressed.

Hope prayed that Ryan didn't notice how her quivering intensified as he shed each article of clothing. *Oh, Lord, help me.* "What do you think you're doing?"

"I want to make love to you." With one knee resting on the bed, Ryan offered his hand—palm up—to Hope. She placed her hand in his and sat on the bed. "I need you, Hope."

She closed her eyes, waited for his kiss, responded to his touch. When he unbuttoned her blouse, she gently touched his hand.

"I can't do this, Ryan."

As if she'd said nothing, he continued to unbutton her blouse.

"Ryan, I---"

He stopped her verbal resistance with a series of pecks and then a tongue kiss. Hope leaned back. Her eyes took in the splendor of his body. She crossed, uncrossed and then crossed her legs again in an effort to quench the raging fire.

"I'm ovulating so unless you're trying to make another baby," she raised her voice, "get dressed!"

He leaned forward, pulled her close, whispered in her ear. "I promise you won't get pregnant."

"That's what you said the last time." He touched her secret spot. "Ryan!"

"That's it; say my name."

"I'm serious… I can't …I can't do this."

Ryan snatched his pants up, grabbed his shirt off the floor.

"Why not? Why can't we make love? I need to be inside of you."

"Why? What's going on with you?"

The phone rang. Ryan answered. Greg, a mutual friend from college, was on the other line.

Hope said, "Let me talk to Greg."

Ryan shook his head and motioned for Hope to remain silent. She left to use the restroom. By the time she returned, Ryan had hung up the phone.

"That was quick."

"Yeah he just wanted to see where I was."

"Does he know you're here visiting me?"

"No."

"Is that why you wouldn't let me to speak to him?"

"No, it's just that Greg knows me. If he knew I was here with you he'd know something was up."

"Does he have a problem with that?"

"Why can't I make love to you?"

"Don't change the subject. Why would it matter if Greg knew you were here?"

"What time is it?" He glanced at the clock on the nightstand.

"You did it again. It's not late. Why?"

"It's just that I have a lot of work to do so maybe you'd better get going."

"Uh-huh. So what would your workload be like if I had sex with you?"

"It's not like that. I have work to do. It was great seeing you, Hope."

"I wish I could say the same, Ryan." She gathered her belongings.

"Woman, you were the one who brought up our past. I was content with just meeting you for lunch. Then you got all deep on me and I realized just how much I missed you."

"No, I tried to give us closure. What were you trying to give us?"

"I've got a riddle for you."

"I'm in no mood to listen to any stupid riddles."

"Okay, then it's not a riddle; just listen. If you could choose between being the woman who was loved and the woman who was married to a guy who did not love her, who would you choose to be?"

"I'm not sure I follow your question. Are you implying that the woman who is married is not loved by her husband because he loves someone else?"

"Yes."

"And you're asking me who I'd prefer to be?"

"Yes."

"You already know my answer."

"You'd rather be the one who's loved, right?"

"Duh."

"Just remember if or when I get married, you're the one who's loved."

"Ryan, are you married?"

"No, naw naw. I'm just saying if I ever were to get married I would still be in love with you. I just thought that if we had a baby, it would substantiate our tie."

"Interesting concept, but it ain't gonna happen."

Chapter Thirteen

Rafael

Hope struggled to forget Ryan. She occupied her idle time with exercise, shopping and class work. She delved into studying her Bible and spent more time in prayer, but she couldn't shake him.

Amanda's wedding was days away. More pertinent was Rafael's departure to Luke Air Force Base in Phoenix after the ceremony. Hope had orders to join him a month later. Rafael insisted they get married and live a fairytale life. The notion sounded great until Hope's rendezvous with Ryan stirred up dormant feelings.

Rafael, Amanda and Hope arrived at Goodfellow on a Saturday afternoon. Amanda went to Arnold's dorm to help him pack while Rafael and Hope picked up Nicole. The trio proceeded to the base gym in search of Richard.

Nicole said, "Hope, I trust you know what you're doing."

"You're the one who told me to do it in public."

"I know but that man is going to try to kill you. And when he does, girlfriend is running." She gestured like a hitch hiker thumbing for a ride.

"Thanks for the support."

"Don't get cynical with me. I told you not to mess with him in the beginning. Now you have the nerve to come here with your new man, passion marks all on your neck and you want me to have your back. You got me stuck." She pointed to the opposite end of the gym where Richard conducted class. "Go on over there. I'll be waiting right here so I can run for help."

Hope grabbed Rafael's hand. "Maybe I shouldn't do this."

"No, go on, honey. Nicole is just teasing you. Everything will be fine. I got your back."

Rafael and Nicole stood at the entrance as Hope walked over to confront Richard.

"Hello, Richard."

Surprised, Richard smiled, hugged her, planted a wet kiss on her mouth. "Hey, baby. When did you get here? Why didn't you call me?"

Hope wiped her mouth. She pulled out the poster she had blown up, pointed to Mi Ling.

"She's why I didn't call, Richard." Hope took the ring out of her pocket, placed it in the palm of his hand, closed his fingers around it. "It's over. You promised you'd never play me dirty and you lied!"

"Wait a minute now." Richard's demeanor transformed. His lips tightened. His chest heaved. He clinched his fists.

Hope turned to walk away but he yanked her by the shoulder; the same shoulder he once caressed.

"I said wait!"

"Get off of me, Richard!" She pulled her military-issued gun from the small of her back and placed it at Richard's head. "You have lost your mind!" She emphasized every syllable. "If you ever touch me again, I promise I will kill you!"

Hope tried to pull away but Richard refused to back down. He moved to stand toe-to-toe with his nemesis. She followed his movement with the gun.

"You gonna kill me, Hope? Well do what you gotta do. I'm not one of these punk airmen. Messing around with me will get you hurt." He stared down the nose of the gun.

Hope looked away in contemplation of her next move.

In a stealth motion, Richard dropped, spun around and grabbed Hope by the neck. He tilted her head to scrutinize the passion marks. "And what is this mess?"

Stunned by his aptness, Hope lowered the weapon but kept her finger on the trigger. "Keep your hands off of me. All of this belongs to that Latin Papí next to Nicole."

He released his grip.

Hope ran her free hand down her body with a subtle hip gyration. "Holla atcha girl! Good bye, Richard. Hope you have a nice life…pun intended." She strutted across the gym with a little extra sway in her prance. She looked like a model sashaying down the runway.

Nicole laughed. "Girlie got heart. I am impressed. Didn't think you had it in you."

"Me neither. He just took me there; carrying on like that when he cheated on me." She turned to Rafael and slapped her hands on her hips. "And why did you let him choke me up like that?"

"How was I supposed to know what he would do? By the time I realized he'd grabbed you, I took a couple steps, but you handled it."

"You can't be mad at Rafael. It happened so fast. He had your back. You better be happy he didn't leave your crazy butt there. I would've."

"Whatever. You are still a nut." She lowered her tone and caressed Rafael's face. "Are we okay, honey? Do you still love me?"

"¿Tú sabes no puedo vivir sin ti?"

"Oh my goodness, Rafael, I have never heard you speak Spanish before."

"You got this man all confused. He doesn't even know what language to speak."

"Quit playing, Nicole. But seriously Rafael, tú no me conoces pero recuerdas que te amo."

"¿El tiempo dira. Tu confias en mi?'

"Yo confio en ti con el corazon roto."

Nicole walked between the two amigos, hooked her arms with theirs, pulled them to the exit. "Aw that's so sweet. Now can one of you freaking Spanish speakers translate for this ghetto sista? I no speaka da Spanish."

"Rafael is going to stay with me because he trusts me and loves me."

"Hmm, then he's crazy, too."

"Give me a hug, girl. It was good seeing you again."

"It was good seeing you, too. Rafael, it was nice meeting you, sexy. Try to keep my friend out of trouble."

"I'll try."

Rafael and Hope reconnected with Amanda and Arnold, then off to Abilene, Texas. Rafael and Hope shared a hotel room despite the flurry of emotions that ran rampant between them. Foolish. The liberation of confronting Richard intensified sexual desire and they obliged the urges almost every hour. If only they were as faithful to God's command of abstinence as they were to defiant acts of simulated procreation. Both consummators knew their affair was unacceptable to the Lord; however they couldn't—or wouldn't—see past the passionate lust. Rafael intrigued Hope beyond her wildest imaginations. Only God could set them free from this raw bondage.

After a series of close encounters throughout the night, Rafael and Hope prepared for the wedding. Hope stood in front of the mirror styling her hair. He zipped up her royal blue dress.

"You look so beautiful." He wrapped his arms around her waist, kissed the nape of her neck. "It should be us getting married today."

She glared at him through the mirror. "Are you serious?

"Very serious. I would marry you right now."

"That's crazy. Are you sure you're not mesmerized by dreams of your father? It's not wise to make life decisions based on quirky dreams."

"Is that what you think? I want you because of my father?"

"You do take your dreams about him to another level. I'm not trying to be insensitive," she swallowed hard then continued, "but your father is dead. Communicating with him is not normal. The Bible even warns us against it. It's not of God." The hypocrisy in her words jolted Richard's treble.

"Then what is of God, Hope? Running around pulling guns on ex-fiancés, screwing in the back of my truck or my personal favorite; almost getting arrested for public sex acts? Was that of God? Face it, our sin separated us from Him a long time ago. That's what makes us matchless. Don't over analyze it. Why can't you just live and be happy?"

"Because this is not living. We're suffocating each

other."

"Tell me what you want me to do."

"Give me room to breathe."

The phone rang. Anxious Amanda called to confirm that they were ready to meet in the lobby.

They carpooled to the courthouse. Rafael and Hope were the only witnesses to the ceremony. With his head tilted and his eyes glassy, Rafael looked like a lost puppy as he watched Arnold and Amanda exchange vows. His occasional sighs infuriated Hope. With only five people in the judge's chamber, his envy was exponential; his light-brown eyes turned green.

After the ceremony, they went to Cocolo's. The bootleg restaurant had lop-sided tables stabilized with newspapers. None of the chairs matched; not an intentional effort of eclectic interior design.

Hope tipped her chair forward to allow the remnants of a previous patron's meal to settle on the floor. Instead of sitting next to her, per the usual routine, Rafael sat catty-corner to make the newlyweds a barrier to communication. He managed to pout and chew at the same time. Amanda broke the silence.

"You two have been sulking ever since we left the hotel. What's up with that?"

Hope looked at Rafael. When he didn't answer, she said, "Nothing, we just realized tonight is our last night together for a while."

"Cheer up and live in the moment. Today is a happy occasion!"

"Hope doesn't think she wants to marry me."

"Rafael, please …it's their special day."

"Is that true, Hope?"

"Not completely." Hope shook her head.

"It better not be. We have to stick to the plan and live in Phoenix together. Don't be stupid, girl."

"I won't, Mandy."

Arnold took a swig of champagne. "Quit ganging up on Hope. I'm sure you two will work everything out."

"Thanks, Arnold."

"No problem. Now let's celebrate with a toast, to the happy couple…salud!"

Later that night, they returned to the hotel.

"Hope why are you trying to pick a fight with me?"

"I'm not."

"Then what are you trying to prove?"

"For starters, I want you to recognize that we do not have a relationship outside of sex."

"Yes we do. It's just this is our last night together for at least a month."

"You just don't get it, do you? We get so sucked in by physical arousal that we have no idea if we love each other or just the sex."

"I love you, Hope. Come on, honey, don't do this to me now."

"Can't you just hold me?"

"Are you kidding? It's impossible to just hold you in my present state." He looked down, pointed to his elevated genitalia.

"That's what I'm talking about. If our connection is only physical, then we have no substance. Without substance, either of us could easily be replaced."

"Trust me; you could never be replaced. You got my mind twisted. I love you, honey...please."

And in a matter of seconds, they imitated horny hares.

Hope drove Rafael to the airport early the next morning. The bitter-sweet departure left Hope in tears. Rafael cried too.

Hope returned to the hotel to check out and chauffeur her passengers back to Goodfellow. They dropped Arnold off and the ladies continued to Sheppard.

A week later, Amanda left for Phoenix which left Hope alone to sort out the residue of Rafael. At first they talked on the phone daily. Then after a few weeks, the communication dwindled to weekly. Hope sensed that something was wrong, but before she had time to worry, Mica called with orders to Sheppard.

"Hope, it's Mica."

"Hey, honey."

"How are you?"

"Wonderful, now that you have orders to Sheppard."

"My plane lands in Dallas tomorrow at 0700. Can you pick me up?"

"Talk about quick. Of course I can pick you up!"

"Do you miss me?"

"You know I do!"

"I'm not going to keep you since we have the rest of our lives together."

"Do you really believe that?"

"Hope, what's wrong?"

"I'm fine, why do you ask?"

"Seems like you're emotionally preoccupied."

"No, honey, I'm okay. I'll see you tomorrow."

"I love you, girl!"

"I love you, too, Mica."

Chapter Fourteen

André

Hope's recent confrontations smothered her anticipation of seeing Mica. She contemplated whether to tell him about Rafael, the lunch with Ryan and the stand off with Richard. She needed the advice of a man, so she called her best friend, André.

Dré—the name that only Hope was allowed to address him by—was the one man she trusted to give her sound advice without an ulterior motive. Their platonic relationship was saturated with emotional intimacy. Hope helped him through a difficult divorce and he carried her across the burning sands of failed relationships and emotional breakdowns. Dré's brutal honesty balanced Hope's out-of-control life. His transparency refreshed her wayward soul; the resonance of his familiar voice brought serenity.

"Hey, Dré, you busy?"

"Nope, what's up?"

"I've got drama."

"So what's new? What's his name?"

"What makes you think it's a guy?"

"Because I know you. In fact it's probably more than one guy."

"Anyway, do you remember Mica?"

"He's still in the game? That's impressive."

"You act like I'm promiscuous."

"You are. How many guys have you been with just in the last year? Even better, how many guys in just the past six months?"

"It isn't as bad as it sounds. I've only been with five guys my entire life. Not to mention I've never had an STD."

"God's hand of protection—not your moral actions—kept you disease free."

"Why do I put up with you?"

"Because you love me and trust I have your best interest at heart."

"So you say. Back to my dilemma, Mica received orders to Sheppard."

"That's great. The problem is?"

"I've been in two other relationships since we were separated. The first I confessed and the other he knows absolutely nothing about. I'm not sure I want to trouble him with the details."

"You think?"

"Give me a break will you?"

"Hope, I'm not going to baby you. That's what's wrong with you now. Everyone caters to your ego which only enables you to remain a spoiled brat. I love you too much to allow you to play yourself so listen to the voice of reason not sympathy. You screwed up again and now you have a choice to make. Either be honest and tell Mica the truth or be deceptive and hide it from him. If he forgave your mess once, what makes you think he wouldn't do it again?"

"I don't want him to have to do it again."

"Then stop screwing around. You complain about how these guys keep cheating on you, but what do you call what you do to Mica?" He paused for Hope's reply, but it didn't' come. "You make simple things so complex. By the way, are you taking into account the emergence of promiscuity?"

"Thanks, Dré, make me feel even worse than I already do."

"Well you aren't exactly the victim here. If you really love this guy you should tell him the truth."

"And if he leaves me?"

"You had it coming. Besides he would not be the first to leave you. But if he stays, maybe this poor buddy really is the one. Either way you'll survive."

"I guess you're right."

"Trust me. Have I ever steered you wrong?"

"Okay but there's still more drama."

"I'm not surprised… keep going."

"I saw an old friend and he's got me second guessing my life."

"Hope, who did you see now?"

"Promise not to get mad."

"No, I'm getting mad waiting for you to tell me."

"Okay fine, I saw Ryan….but the only thing we did was kiss, I promise. But if he'd had his way, I'd be pregnant with his baby again."

"What do you mean pregnant again and when did you see Ryan? Please tell me years ago."

"A few months ago and the pregnancy is a lengthy story. I'll explain in depth later. Why does it matter when I saw him anyway?"

"Uh maybe because I attended Ryan's wedding a little

over a year ago."

"You attended *my* Ryan's wedding and you're just now telling me?"

"He's not *your* Ryan anymore."

"What do you mean? You don't even like Ryan. Do you know his wife?"

"That doesn't matter."

"It matters to me. All the years we've been friends, we've never kept secrets. I'm at a loss for words."

"Apparently we have kept secrets; case in point, your pregnancy."

Hope paused, sighed, blurted, "Fine! I got pregnant back in college with Ryan's baby. I put off telling him until I had to, but that time never came." Her voice quivered, words softened. "I had a miscarriage. I carried that secret around until about a month ago when I confessed to Ryan."

"Did you sleep with him?"

Her tone stiffened. "No, I did not, but he tempted me, Dré. He was butt-naked begging me to sleep with him. When I say I ran away, I truly ran away. So this marriage thing makes no sense. He said that he wanted to be connected to me forever. He even acted like he still wanted to marry me. That's crazy, right?"

"Beyond crazy, it's inexcusable. Speaking of inexcusable; I'm sorry I kept Ryan's wedding from you. We shouldn't keep secrets. I was wrong. I apologize."

"Forget about it. I kept a secret, too. Now get back to pacifying me as my world slowly comes undone."

"Not to add insult to injury but what did Ryan say about the baby?"

"He made jokes about me being his baby's mama and

begged me to allow him to make another one."

"You always pick the most unstable guys. Have you ever dated a guy that wasn't cuckoo for Cocoa Puffs?"

"I think not."

"Well Ms. Tolliver, after the intense emotional roller coaster you've been on, are you sure you want to be with Mica?"

"Yes, I love him."

"Are you sure?"

"Yes. Why? Does it bother you that I might settle down?"

"No, should it?"

"I don't know. It's just that you've been my only constant for so long you might be a little uncomfortable with the notion of sharing me."

"I have never had to share you with any of your men. Our relationship is one-of-a-kind and you know it. Don't compare me to relationships with your flunkies."

"Whatever, Dré. Just tell me how to handle this Ryan situation."

"I'm speechless. You know I love you, but Ryan is married to my colleague, Danielle, regardless of the fact that he's still in love with you."

"Are you ever going to let that go? People do make mistakes."

"Okay but who was the mistake you or Danielle? It's a rhetorical question because Ryan never got over you. The baby just complicates things even more. How did you end up hooking up that day anyway?"

"He called me out of the blue and we went from there."

"Do you think I should tell Danielle?"

"No, Ryan said that he told her all about me. If she still wanted to marry him after knowing he loved me more, then that's on her."

"I don't believe he ever told her. He just lied to make you feel better. Don't forget he neglected to tell you that he was married."

"So you wanted him to say, 'Thanks for telling me we had a baby that died oh and by the way I'm married?'"

"He should have told you the truth. Period. I need you to do something for me."

"If it's worse than finding out Ryan's married, I ain't doing it."

"It's probably equally painful."

"Dré, you can't be serious!" She took the phone from her ear, counted to five.

"You there?"

At ten, she said, "I'm sorry… go on."

"Remember Tommy or whatever you choose to call him these days?"

"Unfortunately I'll never forget him, why?"

"He's been depressed lately. Don't get me wrong, I still hate his guts but…"

"Spit it out, man."

"Despite his most recent divorce, his sister, Misha, seems to think it has more to do with the incident that transpired between the two of you."

"What incident? Oh, my fault is that what his people are calling rape these days? Why are you bringing this up? Wasn't my situation with Ryan traumatizing enough?"

"No and I'm not trying to hurt you. Misha has been asking me to have you talk to him for a while now. I told her you weren't ready, but if you want closure it might be time to heal."

"Are you serious?"

"I think it might help, Hope. I wouldn't bring him up if I didn't."

"Do you want me to call him tonight, tomorrow, next week? Which is better for you?"

"You don't have to be cynical. Whenever you feel the urge let me know. Misha is desperate for him to get better."

"I'm sure she is but how did she feel when he raped me? Forget her. I'll be the bigger person. What's the number?"

"No. You can't call him tonight. You aren't emotionally ready."

"Wrong. Tommy's been tormenting me far too long. What's the number before I lose my nerve?"

"It's 333-5555. Let me know how it goes."

"Sure, Dré. I hope Misha's worth it."

"How did you know we were dating?"

"You better be to put me out there like this."

"Are you mad at me?"

"Does it matter?"

"I'll say a prayer for you. Hope, if you really believe in God, give it to Him and let Him work everything out for you. He will."

"You are definitely dating Misha. She took me to church and has made you a better person."

"Love ya', Hope!"

"Love you, too, Dré."

Chapter Fifteen

Tommy

Hope paced the floor. She couldn't believe that she had agreed to confront her past to appease Dré. After twenty minutes of bantering with herself, she picked up the receiver.

A groggy voice answered, "Hello?"

"Tommy."

"Hope? Hope, is that you?"

"Yes. How are you?"

Tommy sighed, paused. A faint sob channeled through the telephone. "I'm better now. Oh my goodness I didn't think I'd ever hear your voice again. How are you?"

"I'm good."

"I don't know what I did to deserve this call but I'm extremely grateful."

"I heard that you weren't doing well so I called to see if there's anything I can do to help."

"Yes, I uh," he paused. "I know that I really hurt you a few years ago. I did a terrible thing and I'm sorry. Not a day goes by that I don't think about how bad I screwed up. Can you ever forgive me?"

"Apology accepted. I'm sorry that you've been tormenting yourself over this. We all make mistakes so let it go and move on. I forgave you a while ago so now you've got to forgive yourself."

"My punishment is loving you so much that I feel like I'll die without you, but knowing that I'll never be with you again. It hurts more than I can explain."

"I don't want you to hurt, Tommy. Believe me I know what it's like and I wouldn't wish it on my worst enemy; not even you."

"I deserved that."

"I probably shouldn't have called."

"No, I'm happy that you did. You have no idea how much this means to me."

"Uh-huh. I've got to go now."

"Okay. I love you so much, gorgeous."

"Good talkin---"

"Hope, before you go…"

"Yes, Tommy?"

"Do you ever wonder what it would've been like had we gotten married?"

"I used to wonder all of the time."

"I still wonder; I wonder every day. What would our children have looked like? Where would we have lived?"

"It's time to stop wondering and move on."

"I tried to move on but it ended in divorce."

"I'm sorry. Any kids?"

"I have a son. I'm staying in his life and I'll continue to take care of my ex-wife. I'll always care about her, but we just didn't work out."

"I know how that goes."

"I love you so much, Hope. Why didn't we work things out?"

"I love you, too." Hope bit her lip to stifle the downpour of emotions. She had forgiven Tommy but never figured out how to stop loving him. "For starters, you didn't believe in God."

"That's not true." Tommy's voice elevated. "I believe in God I just don't believe in spending every waking hour in church and kicking out the kind of money you paid." He took a deep breath, lowered his voice. "It was like they had you brainwashed. Whenever you talked about religion you sounded like a robot; quoting the Bible like a tent-meeting preacher. You didn't use your own words."

"Now I understand the meaning of an educated fool. Here you are, a doctor without a relationship with the true healer. I'll keep praying for your salvation and your soul. That's true love."

"What does praying for me have to do with loving me?"

"I love you too much to give up on your soul. Someone prayed me through and I'm grateful."

"Are you done yet? We were doing well before you started with your religious nonsense."

"That's why we couldn't work things out, Tommy. God knew that we'd be unequally yoked."

"Now I'm supposed to believe that God controlled our relationship?"

"Yes. As good as you think we may have been for each other, you were not God's perfect will for me. My Father had someone better."

"What are you talking about? Your dad loves me. I keep in touch with him to this day."

"I'm talking about my heavenly Father."

"Here we go again."

"Tommy, we aren't going anywhere and neither is this conversation."

"Let me guess; you need a mighty man of God to be your husband. Not a highly paid doctor, right?"

"No, my husband could be a highly paid doctor, but he has to be a mighty man of God first."

"You're dad was right about you; you're a flake."

"My Father was right about you; you're not the one for me. Goodbye, Tommy."

Hope smiled as she placed the receiver on the carriage. She faced her fear, confronted her assailant and came out on top. She wiped her feet on the carpet, stomped a couple of times and ran herself a hot bubble bath.

Chapter Sixteen

Rafael

With the bath water still soothing Hope's body, the phone rang. She thought about letting it roll over to the answer machine but decided against it. She grabbed a towel, wrapped it around herself, tiptoed across the vinyl floor to the phone.

A woman with a strong Spanish accent spoke broken English.

"May I speak to Hope?"

"This is Hope."

"Pues, I'm Marisol and I'm pregnant."

"Congratulations, but I think you have the wrong number. I don't know anyone named Marisol."

"Su boyfriend es mi boyfriend, too."

"What are you talking about? Is your boyfriend Mica or Rafael?"

"Sí, Rafael."

"Rafael Rodriguez?"

"¿Sí, estás bien?"

Hope breathed a sigh of relief. Had it been Mica, she would have wrapped that towel around her neck like a noose. "Yes, I'm okay. Rafael is not my boyfriend."

"He told me you were his señorita but I'm carrying his niño."

"That's great. Did Rafael give you my number?"

"Sí."

"Is he there with you now?"

"Sí, estás aqui."

"Put Mr. Aficionado on the phone por favor."

"Hey, baby, how are you? I miss you."

"Is that all you have to say to me? Better yet, is Marisol the reason you neglected to call?"

"Hope I...I don't know where to begin."

"How about the beginning?"

"Marisol is my ex-girlfriend. I went home on leave and found out she was pregnant with my baby."

"Let me get this straight; Marisol is your ex-girlfriend and she's pregnant. How do you know it's your baby? Even if you were dating her up until you left, she'd have to be at least seven months."

"Yeah, eight months to be exact."

"Eight months? How didn't you know?"

"Ask Ryan that same question."

"That was dirty on so many levels. So are you marrying her after the baby is born or before?"

"Now you've got jokes. I don't want to marry her; I want to marry you. I know it sounds awful but she means nothing to me. I need you to believe that. Papí said that you were the one and I honestly can't see myself with anyone but you."

"So even though this woman is pregnant you want to abandon her to marry me, and I'm supposed to consider that a good thing? You repulse me. This is precisely why I didn't tell Ryan about my pregnancy. I refused to give him the opportunity to reject me the way you're rejecting Marisol."

"I'm not rejecting her. She's my ex as in completely finished...no mas. She's only staying with me for the time being so I can help her with the pregnancy."

Hope made a screech noise like a car slammed to a quick stop. "Wait! Back up! Rewind! She's staying with you, too?"

"Yes, but I sleep on the sofa. I'm tired of talking about this. That's the reason I told her about us. I'm trying to make her understand that I don't want her; I want to be with you!"

"Do you really want me or is this your dead father talking again? I'm not trying to be insensitive but you're not thinking rationally."

"I'm trying to do the right thing. I'm rejecting Marisol not the baby."

"Did you ever stop to consider her feelings or is everything about you?"

"Is this coming from Ms. I-still-can't-tell-Ryan-I-had-a-miscarriage?"

"You are way out of line Rafael and to reciprocate testing your ego; I told Ryan about our baby and he begged me to allow him to create another."

"You told Ryan about the baby? When?"

"While you and I were dating. How's it feel, you jerk? I'm trying to put my feelings aside to think about what's best for everyone involved. Make an effort to do the same."

"You know I don't believe in abortions so I'm allowing her to have our child. That doesn't mean I have to marry her."

"Well aren't you the saint? Don't you realize why this is so personal to me? I was Marisol not too long ago. She loves you, Rafael. Don't you see that?"

"Papí never liked her. He said she wanted to trap me." He paused. "Looks like he was right."

"She's carrying your seed. Doesn't that mean anything to you?"

"This isn't fair. I'm not in love with Marisol. I'm in love with you."

"Wake up! I loved you, too; our crazy excursions, the way you made me feel. But this predicament confirms that we were never meant to be anything more than we were. It was what it was; nothing more, nothing less."

"I can't...I can't let you go."

"You will in time."

"But you and I were on a different level than most."

"You'll exceed that level with Marisol. She is having your baby; something I may not have ever been able to give you. Our lives have changed. It's foolish to try to hold on to the past when we've already seen a glimpse of the future."

"I know I messed up but do I have to suffer for the rest of my life from one mistake?"

"Your child is not a mistake. Just pray. Make sure you pray God's perfect will and not your own. Everything will work out fine."

"This is about your past with Ryan not my present, isn't it?"

"Possibly…in any event, focus on Marisol."

"What about her?"

"I'm sure at some point you loved her."

"I did but not anymore. Besides, you and I never got a chance to say goodbye."

"Yes we did; we just didn't know it at the time."

"I love you, Hope. Please don't walk away from us."

"I love you, too, Rafael. That's why I'm letting you go."

"I am not Tommy, Ryan or Richard, so why are you running away from me?"

"It's what I do. It's what I've become accustomed to. Let's wrap this up before I start crying."

"Wait, one more thing?"

"Yes, Rafael?"

"Promise me that every time you look up at the stars at night you'll remember I'm staring at them…thinking of you?"

"Didn't I say enough? Are you trying to make me cry?"

"Just promise me...please? It would mean a lot to me."

"I promise."

"I love you, Hope."

"Goodbye, Rafael. Take care."

Chapter Seventeen

Richard

Just as the phone hit the cradle, it rang again. Afraid of who was lurking behind door number three, Hope stared at the phone. Still damp from her interrupted bubble bath, a chill raised goose bumps on her arms. Curiosity got the best of her.

"Hello?"

"Hey, baby, are you asleep?"

"No, unfortunately I am wide awake. Richard?"

"Yes?"

"What do you want?"

"I just called to check on you."

"Why?"

"I still think about you a lot. Is that a crime?"

"I'm tired. What do you need, want, whatever? For once in your pathetic existence be honest with me. I'm too worn out to deal with your perplexity."

"I thought you said you weren't asleep?"

"I wasn't but I'd like to get there some time soon. It's after eleven and I have a lot to do tomorrow."

"Like what?"

"Like none of your business. Richard, are you sick?"

"No."

"Is anyone in your family hurt?"

"Not to my knowledge."

"Then goodnight."

"Hope, please can I have just one minute? I need to talk to you."

"About what, Richard? What could we possibly have left to talk about?"

"I couldn't help but notice your boy, Mica, received orders to Sheppard."

"You have to be kidding me. You refuse to let it go. You've reduced yourself to stalking my man? That is a little excessive even for you."

"Okay, I'll be a stalker but what's Taco Bell going to think about Mica?"

"Probably the same thing I thought about Mi Ling."

"Touché."

"Ya think? His name is Rafael not Taco Bell and he won't be thinking anything about Mica. He and I are no longer together."

"Wow, you didn't waste any time with that one."

"Not that it's any of your business, but he found out his ex-girlfriend was pregnant."

"She's pregnant with his baby?"

"You in the habit of repeating now?"

"And he just left you high and dry?" Richard laughed.

"You wish. I rejected his marriage proposal which forced him to do the right thing. Something your heart knows nothing about. I don't need this aggravation. I'm getting off the phone."

"No wait, baby. Everybody's not okay."

"Who's hurt?"

"I am, seriously. I've been in a dark place since you left me."

"Excuse me? What did you just say? Don't you mean since you cheated on me?"

"Yes, since I cheated but I miss you. So naturally when I saw Mica's orders, I panicked."

"Does that give you the right to stalk him?"

"I've paid attention to his assignments not stalked him. Don't worry, I'm not Tommy. You just make me do crazy things."

"Tommy said the exact same thing. Maybe I do drive men crazy. You all insist that you were sane prior to me and I seem to be the only common denominator."

"No, I think you just attract undercover psychos."

"Including you?"

"I guess. You see me bothering you, desperate like Boo Boo the Fool in love. So are you and Mica trying to work things out?"

"Again none of your business."

"Does he know about me?"

"Yes, I told you that at Goodfellow!"

"Ooh, you are appalling. You act like we have no history; like I'm some bum on the street. Hell has no fury like a woman scorned."

"That's interesting. You're not the first man to call me appalling. I guess I'll put that on my relationship resume next to will drive you insane. Richard, I forgive you and prayerfully I will be able to forget all the hurt and pain you inflicted. Until then, stay out of my life!"

"No, I can't promise that. I was hoping you would consider giving me another chance, if things don't work out with Mica."

"Over the years I've learned to refrain from the use of the word *never*…but don't hold your breath."

"Have I made you this bitter and cynical?"

"Don't flatter yourself. You don't have nor did you ever have that kind of power over me. My guard remains up when I don't trust someone. You of all people should know that being intelligence operations. Perhaps you were asleep when they taught us clandestine behavior and covert operations. Just be happy I didn't kill you when I busted you with Mi Ling because, make no mistake, you were unquestionably my enemy that night."

"You are trippin', baby."

"How many times are you going to call me baby? I am not Mi Ling. By the way how is she?"

"I wouldn't know. Furthermore I don't care."

"That's too bad. You threw my love away for someone you don't even care about."

"I see this is going nowhere so I will let you go. Stay in touch if you can."

"I'll think about it."

"I hope to hear from you soon."

"Uh-huh. Goodbye."

Hope hung up the phone feeling as if she'd taken three steps back. She forgave Tommy, the rapist, so why was she unforgiving toward Richard? She knew that true forgiveness was to act as if the offense never happened. She held on to the pain Richard caused. Why? Could it be that Richard was a constant reminder of how Christ saw her? His image of her beauty conflicted with Hope's view of herself. The quandary allowed her to dismiss Richard without much effort.

Chapter Eighteen

Mica

The next morning, Hope crawled out of bed. Her weary body couldn't conjure up enough momentum to live out the excitement she had about seeing Mica. In the years that separated them, every aspect of Hope had changed; her emotions, her perspective on life, even her appearance. Her toned body and tight gluts were a result of years of dedication to physical discipline. Too bad she didn't have that same fervor for her inward man.

Given the daily rigors of military life, Hope often sported Air Force issued uniforms and pulled her hair back in a pony tail. Committed to impressing Mica, she decided to treat herself to a mini makeover. She scoured through the Yellow Pages for a salon.

"I really need this beautician to be a magician." She simulated pulling a rabbit out of a top hat. "Presto chango, you're beautiful and all for fifty bucks."

Hope arrived at the salon about 9:30 am. The strip-mall shop had three beauticians and a nail technician who doubled as the receptionist.

"Good morning, my name is Shakena. How can we help you today?"

"I need a cut, wash and set, ASAP!"

"Yes, ma'am. Arvena can take you at the first station."

Hope looked at her nails. "How much do you charge?"

"I'm running a special this week. Manicure and pedicure for twenty-five dollars."

"Perfect."

Less than three hours later, Hope was transformed. She tipped the stylist and manicurist, bounced out of Linda J's Salon. The products made her hair smell wonderful and flow free in the gentle breeze.

The quick service gave Hope ample time to grab a sandwich before her massage. The expert masseuse had a large client base and was adamant about timeliness. Whenever Hope arrived late, she deducted the time from her scheduled hour, but required full payment. Few clients arrived late.

Hope left the spa around 2:00 pm refreshed and ready to shop for a stunning outfit and sandals. Because she had a rigid timeline to follow, she bumped into her dorm mate, Patricia.

"Hey Patricia. What's up girl?"

"You are, if you're still dating Rafael."

Hope threw her freshly manicured hand on her hip and rolled her eyes. "I'm not and I don't want to discuss him."

"Oh, girl I understand. No need for the 'tude. Can you believe Eric is married?"

Hope tapped Patricia on the shoulder. "Shut up."

"Yes. The entire time we dated he was married."

"How did you find out?"

"He called home to his wife while lying next to me."

"Did he think you were asleep?"

"Who knows? Freaking loser. I almost went to jail that night."

"I know it. Although we might feel justified, no man is

ever worth jail. We deserve so much better."

"Miss Lady, you sure are using a lot of 'we' today. Last time I checked, you weren't dating a married man or were you?"

"No, but I might as well have been. Tricia, Rafael had some girl pregnant back home during our relationship."

"Shut up. Did he know that she was pregnant?"

"I don't think so but who knows? He could have been playing me dirty."

"So you think Eric was playing me dirty?"

"Uh, he was married, so unless he had amnesia, how does that just slip one's mind? Even if Eric and his wife were separated, he was still obligated to tell you."

Patricia nodded. "Yeah, he straight played me dirty. After I confronted him, he had the audacity to assume that I'd go along with it." She lowered her pitch to a pseudo bass. "'You've been committing adultery all of this time, so why stop now?'"

"Uh-huh. I thought I had it bad."

The dorm mates laughed until tears ran down their cheeks.

Patricia snorted, paused to gather herself. "Why do we settle?"

"I don't know." Hope crinkled her forehead. "Did we really settle though? We didn't know they were involved with other people and cut them loose as soon as we found out."

"I think I knew something was up, but didn't want to believe it. Eric altered and cancelled our plans on a regular and I thought little of it."

"I see what you're saying, but being paranoid that someone is playing you is like waiting for the doctor to tell you whether that lump in your breast is benign or malignant. Honey, that is not living. Besides, Rafael and I were attached at the hip. He never cancelled our plans but he did have a baby-in-waiting. I talked to his family on a regular basis and never once did they mention a pregnant ex."

"Well, Rafael may have been different but Eric was definitely a dog. He even has puppies." She snickered. "I mean kids."

Hope chuckled. "That's cute. So why did the Air Force place him in single dorms if he was married?"

"You got me. I guess because his family wasn't living on base."

"And he never mentioned his children?"

"He mentioned *a* child, but he said that he had a baby mama not a wife. And he eluded that their relationship was in the past. He never talked to his wife or kids when we were together and that was quite often."

"That's crazy."

"So are you going to be with Mica now or what?"

"I think so. Richard disqualified himself by cheating on me. Rafael doesn't know how to be honest and I'm not up for stepmomma drama. So that pretty much leaves Mica."

"I'm not an expert at this, but I'm pretty sure you don't choose a man by default. What is wrong with you?"

"That did sound awful, but I didn't mean it like that. Mica has always had my heart."

"I don't think that's all he wants."

"He has always treated me with the utmost respect." Hope smiled, twirled her hair. "He's not like most guys."

"You mean ya'll have never done the nasty?"

Hope raised her voice to early-morning callisthenic level. "No, we have not!" She looked around to see how many people heard her outburst. An older man peered at her over his horn-rimmed spectacles. She lowered her tone, continued, "We were going to once but it didn't work out."

"I knew a brotha that fine had to have a flaw or two or three."

"No, he really doesn't. He decided I was a jewel too precious to disrespect by depositing an illegal seed. He wanted to wait until marriage."

"An illegal what? You sure he isn't gay?"

"No, Patricia. He's a born-again Christian. He believes people should wait until they are married before engaging in sex."

"He's a virgin?"

"No, he's had sex, but that was before he found Jesus."

"So now that he's found Jesus, he won't give you the goods?"

"Am I not speaking your language? No, señorita. Not until we're married."

"Oh, it's like that?"

"Patricia don't you read your Bible?"

"Nope, but if it will get me a man like Mica, I'm starting today."

"You are too crazy. I gotta go. Talk to you later."

"Oh no, Miss Thang! You don't start a conversation like this and refuse to finish it. Have a seat." Patricia motioned for Hope to sit on a bench in the mall.

"I can't talk long. I have to have time to get ready so I can look hot for Mica at the airport."

"What time does his flight arrive?"

"Seven."

"It's only three. Talk to me."

"I don't have a choice, do I?"

"No, you don't." She looked at the empty seat on the bench, back at Hope. She took Hope's hand, pulled her to the bench. "So now let me get this straight. You told Mica all about Richard and Rafael and he still only wants to be with you?"

"It's something like that. I didn't exactly tell him about Rafael."

"But you told him about Richard?"

"Yep."

"And he still wants to be with you?"

"So he says."

"Ooo wee! How do you do what you do? Wait let me get a pen so I can write this stuff down."

"You are silly, Tricia."

"I am serious. I thought I had game but if I looked it up in the dictionary your picture would be right there."

"I don't have any tricks. I've learned to trust God. Everyday He works it out for me."

"Yeah, but who were you trusting when you were bumping and grinding all over the place with Rafael?"

"Thank God for His mercy and His grace."

"So that's it? Just trust God?"

"Yes, but just like any relationship, trust comes from time spent and commitment. What happened when you didn't spend time with Eric?"

"We broke up. I know how to spend time with a man, but how in the world do you spend time with God? Doesn't going to church count for something?"

"Of course He wants us in church, but following man's

expectation is religion. I'm not saying don't go to church, but if you don't know the One you are reverencing, why attend church? You have to know God for yourself. He will lead and guide you into all truth. He wants relationship. How? Praying, fasting, studying His Word, Tricia." Hope noticed the look of bewilderment on Tricia's face. "Instead of going out to eat like you would on a date, set aside time to commune with your first love. For me, a nice hot bubble bath, smooth music and candles set the mood for me to talk with my boo."

"Your boo? That sounds sacrilegious."

Hope giggled. "Not at all. God is a jealous God and He wants my time and attention. He wants me to share my deepest hurts and fondest dreams with Him. He wants to hear my voice whisper His name, not just when I need something, but simply because I love Him."

"Sounds a lot like my men."

"Exactly. The difference is that His love is pure. He wants only the best for you and doesn't want anything from you but your heart." Tears welled in Hope's eyes. "I've spent years chasing after the love of a man only to find that my true love was there all the time; waiting for me to come running to Him. He wants to love me without condition, flaws and all." She looked into Tricia's eyes. "Now tell me that you're not interested in being loved like that."

"You know I think you are fourteen-karat crazy, right? But I'm going to try God and if He works, I'll-I'll, I don't know what I'll do. Is Mica saved?"

"Yes, he's saved and he better stay prayed up to resist hoochies like you."

"I know I ain't right, but are they teaching people to

call women hoochies in church?"

"No, you know I'm kidding." Hope looked at her watch, stood. "I'm happy I stayed to talk to you. Repent and live. You're going to be amazed at how God will use you when you submit to His will."

Tricia laughed. "That's easier said than done. Hope, I'm sincerely happy for you, but I don't think you should marry Mica."

"Why, Patricia? Do you know something I don't?"

"Yes, I want him for myself."

"You're a nut. I really do have to go. If we do get married, I will send you an invitation to the wedding. You better be living right when you get there."

"I'll try but you know how I get down." Patricia stood, gyrated her pelvic as if LL Cool J was her dance partner.

"I love you, girl, but you need Jesus right now."

"I do and I'm going to seek Him for real. Hope, don't stop praying for me."

"I won't. I'll see you."

"Well I hope to see your man with his fine self."

Hope shook her head and rushed away from Patricia. She ran through the mall to get the final pieces for her I-want-my-man-to-salivate-when-he-sees-me look. With the ensemble complete, Hope sped home to shower and dress. She turned on the portable fan next the bathroom sink to keep the perspiration at bay.

Satisfied with her appearance—a fitted black dress which accentuated her curvature, sandals, moderate jewelry to draw attention up to her face and a fresh relaxer—Hope splashed on Mica's favorite cologne, Cashmere Mist by Donna Karan and then zoomed to the airport.

She arrived twenty minutes earlier than anticipated. On her way to the arrival gate, she picked up a newspaper left on a restaurant stool. She folded the paper three times and used it to fan herself.

She mumbled, "I can't have my hair and make-up looking like I just ran a marathon." She paced the waiting area. *Calm down, Hope. Take a deep breath. Hold. Release.* Her futile attempts to relax served only to make her more anxious. She forced herself into an uncomfortable lobby seat, sat on the edge careful to keep her legs crossed.

Preoccupied with the mother and baby across the aisle, Hope didn't notice Mica approach her.

"Well don't just sit there, girl, show me some love."

Hope squealed, leapt from her seat, wrapped her arms around Mica. He dropped to his knee.

"Oh, I'm sorry, Mica. I didn't mean to knock you down. Let me help you up."

He laughed. "Hope, what are you doing? You didn't knock me down." He pulled a ring box from his jacket pocket.

Hope threw her hand over her mouth, fidgeted with her dress, threw her hand over her mouth again.

"Hope Ashley Tolliver, will you marry me?"

Tears cascaded down her cheeks. "Yes, yes, yes! Mica, I'll marry you!"

Although Mica presented Hope with her third proposition, for the first time, she had accepted it with all of her heart. She realized that Mica was the one and the inspiration filled her with peace and contentment. As if surrounded by the romantic night lights illuminating the Eiffel Tower, they kissed with intense fervor.

"Honey, take a deep breathe."

"So you really do love me?" She laid her head on his chest and inhaled his masculinity.

"I told you that I would love you forever."

"And you felt that strongly all of this time? Even in training?"

"Especially in training. I couldn't tell you because it would've scared you away. You had been through so much with men already, I had to prove to you that I was different." He caressed Hope's face, lifted her chin, gazed into her eyes. "No more sharing you with anybody else. If we're going to do this, from here on out it has to be you, me and God."

"Oh, you don't have to worry. I'm all yours."

"Perfect." He kissed her forehead. "I have one more request."

"Anything, baby. What is it?"

"I don't want a lengthy engagement. We've been away from each other too long, so let's set a date as soon as possible."

Hope took a half-step back. "How soon are you talking?"

"How quickly can you plan a wedding?"

"You want to get married that quick, huh? I need at least a month."

"A month would be perfect."

"What about our families? Don't you want them to attend?"

"Works for me. I'll call home and tell Mom. You know my dad died, right?"

"Yeah, I know. I'm so sorry."

"He would've loved you." Mica paused. "On a lighter

note, I'll give you a list of my boys back in New York, so you can send invitations. You know I'm an only child, but do you think your brothers and sisters would want to be a part of the wedding?"

"Of course. I'd like my best friend, Dré, to be my maid of honor. He's a guy, is that going to be a problem?"

"If it makes you happy, I'm down."

"Let's get your luggage so we can talk more about the wedding." Hope stood on her tiptoes, gave him a gentle peck. "I missed you so much."

They rushed back to base. Mica checked into billeting; discounted hotel-like housing for active-duty military members.

"You staying with me tonight?"

"Only if you promise to keep your hands to yourself."

"Still proving myself, huh?" He smiled, pushed the elevator call button. When the door opened, he stepped to the side and said, "After you, milady."

"Why thank you, your highness."

At the room, Mica dropped the bags, plopped on the queen-sized bed. "Whew! I'm exhausted. Flying does something to the body." He closed his eyes.

Hope stared at her man sprawled out on the bed. His body more tone than she remembered. The muscles in his arms and thighs swelled through his clothes. His chocolate skin, flawless. "Lord, help me to hold out."

"You say something?"

"Oh, no. Just yawning."

"I'm going to take a quick shower."

"Okay. I'll call Mommy." Hope exhaled, picked up the receiver, placed it back on the carriage. "Lord, I know it's last minute, but please let my family and friends be able to attend the wedding." She dialed.

"Hello, Mommy?"

"Hope?"

"Yes, ma'am. Guess what."

"What did you do, child?"

"I'm getting married."

"What? Richard called and told me that the wedding was off because you left him for some Mexican."

"Mommy, his name was Rafael and I did not leave Richard. He cheated on me. None of that matters, I'm marrying Mica."

"You found someone else to marry so soon? That's a rebound move. Are you pregnant?"

"No, Mommy, I'm not pregnant."

"Then what's the hurry. Is he an illegal?"

"Mommy, no! Will you just listen to me?"

"I'm trying, Hope, but you come up with some crazy stuff."

"Remember when I was in training and I hung out with Mica Campbell on Thanksgiving?"

"Yeah, I remember you mentioning him. He's the one you left for Richard, right?"

"Mommy, can we please stop talking about Richard?"

"Okay, go on."

"Well he's the guy."

"I thought you two were assigned to different bases."

"We were but not anymore, and once we're married we'll have the same orders everywhere we're stationed."

"Well it seems as though you have your mind made up. Have you set a date yet?"

"July thirteenth."

"Of what year?"

"This year, Mother."

"Hope, that's less than a month away."

"I'm aware of that, Mommy. Can you make it?"

"I don't know. Your sister has a college tour that I'm chaperoning. Maybe your godmother can stand in for me. She lives there in Dallas."

"Are you serious? Of course you are. What on earth was I thinking?"

"Don't start your whining. I'll try Hope but I can't promise you anything. You make rash decisions and then expect everyone to drop everything to cater to your whim."

"I know it's short notice but it's my wedding, Mommy. I need you here with me." Hope sighed. "I don't know why I expected your support. You didn't even come to my graduation from training."

"I told you that I didn't have the money."

"I know, but you have money to take Abby on this college tour. I'll talk to you soon. Love you."

"Okay. Don't forget to call your godmother."

"Yes, ma'am."

Hope hung up the phone. Absence from her mother had not made the heart grow fonder. She was the same old Sarah. Oh well. Hope knew that Nicole would appreciate the news, so she called her.

"Nicole?"

"Hope?"

"What's up girl? How have you been?"

"Great. What are you doing on the thirteenth of next month?"

"What day of the week is that?"

"It's a Saturday."

"Nothing as far as I know. What's going on?"

"Mica proposed to me!"

"Girl, shut up."

"Aren't you excited for us?"

"Yes, that's great and I will definitely be there."

"Can you be in the wedding?"

"Heck yeah." After a sufficient pause, Nicole said, "Hope, you sure you love him?"

"Yes, I really do."

"So you're over Richard?"

"What is it with Richard? Yes, as over him as I'll ever be."

"What about that Jay Hernandez clone you brought here with you?"

"I'm over him, too. He's got a baby on the way by his ex."

"I didn't ask you that. My question was simple: Are you over him?"

"Yes. Good Lord."

"Are you sure? He was a fine ol' something."

"So is Mica."

"I know but... well, you know what you want."

"That's right and it's Mica."

"Put that fool on the phone."

"He's in the shower."

"That's what I'm talking about, girl. Ya'll finally handled ya business."

"No, we didn't."

"You have got to be kidding me."

"We're going to wait until we are married. It's only a month away so why not wait?"

"A month can feel like forever. It was different when

you were separated but seeing him everyday, humph. Do you think you can refrain?"

"Not by ourselves but with God's help all things are possible. I think it's neat that he loves me enough to wait."

"Oh, so since Richard didn't kill your butt, you decided to find Jesus?"

"I had Jesus, quit playing. You used to go to church with me remember?"

"Anyone can go to church but everyone does not have a personal relationship with God like Mica does."

Hope scoffed. "What we have is real."

"And I am sincerely happy for you. It sounds like he's really the one. I can't wait to tell Daddy. He's going to flip when I tell him that his stone-cold brick house is getting married."

"He'll be all right."

"You need any help with anything?"

"Nope, not yet, just get here. I'll mail you the details soon."

"So I finally get to meet Ms. Sarah."

"I doubt it. Please change the subject."

"She'll be there. Don't worry. She will not miss her daughter's wedding."

"Thanks, Nicole. Love you, girl!"

"Uh-huh, you better. Talk to ya soon and congratulations again!"

"Thank you. See you later."

Hope hung up the phone, smiled. Assuring Nicole of her decision to marry Mica gave her reassurance. The chat left her a little more optimistic about pulling off the ceremony. "I need to see if the bookstore has *How to Plan*

a Wedding in Thirty Days or *Weddings for Dummies.*"
Hope laughed, snapped her fingers. "Gotta call André."

"Hey, Dré, it's Hope. Were you busy?"

"Yes, but I'm never too busy for you. What's up?"

"I'm getting married and I want you to be my maid of honor."

"You're what? Who are you marrying? When? And what kind of fruity stuff would that be for me to be your maid of honor?"

"To Mica on July thirteenth, next month."

"Why? Are you pregnant?"

"No and why does everyone keep asking me that?"

"Because once again, Hope, you are doing things jacked up as usual."

"Dré, do I detect a slight attitude?"

"No, I'm happy for you. Just explain the maid of honor thingy."

"You're my best friend, right?"

"Yeah, I better be."

"Well that spot is for the best friend of the bride, traditionally a female. You don't have to wear a dress, unless you want to."

"Not funny."

She giggled. "I had to get that one in. You'll wear a tux, but instead of standing with the groomsmen, you'll be standing next to me and the other bridesmaids."

"Only for you, Hope. Only for you."

"Excellent. Two out of three isn't bad."

"Who said 'no'?"

"My dear, sweet, Mommy."

"That's deep. You'll be all right, you always are."

"I am too happy to let her rain on my parade. Change

the subject please."

"Okay, back to this guy. When do I get to meet him?"

"Judging by our hectic schedules, I'd say at the rehearsal dinner."

"That sucks."

"I know but we still have classes. Contrary to popular belief, this is not Club Med. We're still active duty Air Force members."

"True. Keep me posted and give me exact details."

"Hey, you know me; Ms. Type A personality. You'll be getting the details soon."

"Love you."

"I love you, too. Can't wait to see you!"

Hope hung up the phone. Just as she was about to call Daddy Mark, Mica walked out of the shower with a hotel towel wrapped around his waist. Water glistened on his chest, arms and shampooed mane.

"Ah, that felt good."

"I will have all of the arrangements taken care of by Saturday."

"Are you sure you don't need me to do anything?"

"You can call your boys and family."

"That's all you need me for?"

"I need you for everything, but in regards to the wedding, that's it for now. I'll let you know when you need to get fitted and when we need to sign our marriage license. Other than that, just show up for the rehearsal dinner and the wedding. Oh and I don't want to do the bachelor party thing, if that is okay with you."

"Sure, honey, whatever you want is okay by me. Now come here."

"Okay but don't you want to get dressed first?"

"I just want to hold my fiancé for a minute. Is that alright with you?"

"Yes." She pointed her finger at Mica. "But no funny stuff."

After a sensual hug and kiss, they curled up together on the bed and fell asleep.

~~~~~~~~

Over the next three weeks, Hope ran non-stop orchestrating the flurry of ceremonial specifics. Supportive as usual, Mica often pitched in to help. Surprisingly, all seventy guests managed to RSVP except for one of Mica's friends and Hope's entire family. Even Daddy Mark conjured up a minuscule excuse as to why he couldn't attend.

Mr. and Mrs. Campbell-to-be arranged to exchange vows at The Falls; a beautiful location in Wichita Falls, Texas. The venue offered gazebos and elaborate canopies for outdoor weddings, lavish reception halls and a variety of catered meals. Hope chose the Italian cuisine prepared by the master chef.

Three days before the wedding, Mica's high-school buddies and Nicole arrived. Mica picked them up from the airport and brought them to billeting. Hope waited for them in the lobby.

"Nicole!"

"Hope!"

The friends ran to each other and hugged.

"Oh, Nicole. It's so good to see you. I missed having you around to help me stay focused."

"I thought Lisa and Patricia were helping you with the arrangements. Couldn't handle you, huh?"

"You know it."
~~~~~~~~

They giggled, hugged again.

Mica took Hope by the hand. "Babe, come here. I want you to meet everybody. This is Chris, Vince, Mike and Jason."

"Hi, it's nice to meet you all." Hope looked each guy in the eyes, as she shook his hand. "I know you rode here together from the airport, but I want to introduce you to my good friend and bridesmaid, Nicole."

After the introductions, the guests placed their luggage in the rooms and then the group drove downtown for dinner at Applebee's. As they waited for a table, Vince, the tallest of the bunch, said, "So what are you going to do with your girls tomorrow?"

"I'm sorry, Vince. I don't understand your question."

"You know while we have Mica out doing the bachelor party thing; what are you and your girls going to do? Maybe we can hook up."

Hope looked at Mica. "Honey, I thought we discussed otherwise."

"Mica told us what you decided, but we thought he was joking." Vince elbowed Hope. "Come on, Hope. You can't let our boy go out like that."

Hope furrowed her brow, titled her head, cocked her lip. "Like what?"

"He has to have a bachelor party. It's what real men do."

Nicole interjected. "Hope, just let it go."

"No, Nicole, I will not let it go. Mica, honey do you care to elaborate on these so-called plans?"

Mica looked puzzled, as if he hadn't been following the conversation. "What plans?"

"Whatever plans Vince is talking about?"

"Man, I don't know." He turned to Vince. "I thought I told you guys we were good without a bachelor party."

With a smirk on his face, Vince shrugged.

Mica turned back to Hope. "There's not going to be a party. I promise."

"You swear."

"I pinky swear." He offered his pinky. "No party."

Hope hooked her pinky with Mica's and then smiled.

The hostess escorted the group to a large booth in the back corner. Once the waitress took the meal order and served the drinks, Hope explained the wedding details. She handed out copies of the agenda complete with arrival times, locations and driving directions.

"We have one hour to run through the ceremony. The Falls has several weddings Saturday, so I need everyone there on time." She turned to Mica. "No exceptions."

"What?"

"The guys need to pick up their tuxedoes by four Friday to make dress rehearsal on time. André is having some logistical problems, but he promised to get his tux before the store closed." She sipped the water with lemon through a straw. "The three bridesmaids have already picked up their dresses. The cake, food, flowers and everything else is done. Any questions?" Hope looked at each dinner guest for nonverbal affirmation that she communicated her expectations. "Oh yeah, dinner after the rehearsal will be at Guido's."

The waitress brought Styrofoam containers for leftovers, the wedding party returned to billeting.

The following morning, the party reconvened for breakfast in the hotel dining area. Hope peeled a navel orange as she reviewed her checklist for the day.

Mica leaned over to her. "Whatcha got there?"

Hope grabbed her pen to jot down two more to-do items.

"Hope?"

"Huh?"

"I said, 'Whatcha got there?'"

"Oh, I'm sorry. I didn't hear you." She took a napkin to dab away the juice that squirted onto her blouse. "It's a lis---"

"Can you pick up my mother from the airport? Her flight gets in at eleven and the guys and I still have some things to knock out."

Hope sighed, rolled her eyes, went back to writing notes.

"If it's too much to ask---"

"No, I'll do it. I just have a lot of things to do myself. Plus I've never met your mother. It would be nice if you were there to introduce us."

"I know. I'll make it up to you."

"Uh-huh. You have a lot of making up to do." She forced a smile, turned to Nicole. "Nicole, wi--"

"Let's go."

Hope and Nicole jumped in the car and headed for the airport.

"So you've never met his mother? How awkward is this gonna be?"

"He's told me a lot about her. She sounds like a nice lady."

"Did he tell you what she looked like?"

"No, why?"

"You may need to know what she looks like to pick her up."

"Oh, shoot. Let me call Mica." When he didn't answer his cell phone, Hope said, "He's probably getting his tuxedo. I could make a sign with her name on it, but I don't have any paper. She shouldn't be that tough to spot. He said that she's cute as a button and not much taller than one."

Hope and Nicole stood at baggage claim. They panned the area for likely suspects and approached a couple of candidates. Fifteen minutes into watching the third matriarch, Hope decided to make a move.

"Mrs. Campbell?"

"Yes, dear." She put on the glasses that dangled from a chain around her neck. "Oh darling, come here and give me a colossal hug." Hope took care not to squeeze the feeble-looking woman too hard. "Oh bless your heart, sweetie, bless your heart. Mica mailed me your picture, but you look much thinner in person. You are one beautiful young lady."

"Thank you, Mrs. Campbell. I love you already!"

"Please, dear, call me 'Mom.'" Mrs. Campbell turned her attention to Nicole who fidgeted with the energy of a puppy on display in a pet store. "And you are…?"

"Oh, I'm sorry. Where are my manners? This is my dear friend, Nicole."

Nicole extended her hand. Mrs. Campbell took off her glasses, inspected Nicole, humphed, put on her glasses. Nicole withdrew her hand.

Mrs. Campbell peered at Nicole from over the top of her spectacles. "Are you the maid of honor, dear?"

"No, I'm just a bridesmaid."

"Well, aren't you cute?" She patted Nicole on the top of her head, pointed to the bag on the ground. "Be a dear and get my suitcase."

Nicole looked at Hope, cut her eyes at the little old lady. "Yes, ma'am." She snatched the bag.

"Careful with that."

"Sorry."

"These old legs aren't as strong as they used to be, Marie. Can you walk a few steps behind to catch me in case I stumble?"

Nicole tightened her lips, mumbled under her breath.

"You say something, honey?"

"My name is Nicole."

Hope looked back at Nicole. She mouthed, I'm sorry, shrugged, walked beside Mrs. Campbell.

"Mrs. Campbell, when---"

"Mom, remember?"

"Yes, ma'am. Mom, when we get you settled at the base I thought you might enjoy a day at the spa."

"That sounds wonderful. It's been years since I've been pampered." She looked back at Nicole. "Will Karen be joining us?"

"Nicole."

"Excuse me?"

"Her name is Nicole and yes ma'am, she'll be joining us. It was her idea."

"Humph."

Wrapped in plush terry cloth bathrobes relaxed at the pedicurist's station, Mrs. Campbell talked about Mica's childhood, his father and his life before Hope. She cherished her son and he adored her. An obvious mama's boy, Hope appreciated the job she'd done in raising him so she couldn't complain.

Mrs. Campbell leaned forwarded in the massage chair

and pointed to Nicole's feet. "Marsha, were you born like that or did something happen to cause that deformity?"

"Look here, la---"

"I think Nicole has beautiful feet." Hope pulled her feet out of the water and propped them on the side of the soaking tub. "Now these feet, these are a hot mess." She laughed. "But Mica loves 'em crooked toes and all." She placed her feet back in the warm, bubbling water.

"Yes he does." Mrs. Campbell peered over the top of her glasses. "Kimberly, what kind of manicure did you get? Looks like you've got doo-doo brown confetti splashed all over those long, pointy nails. Look like claws on a rabid dog or something."

Nicole splashed her feet in the water, grabbed a magazine. She placed it inches from her face, spewed silent venomous words onto the pages.

"Mom Campbell, that's how Nicole likes her nails. They fit her personality."

"Well that's a countrified calamity and it's going to make my Mica's wedding a big joke."

"It's *our* wedding and the colors complement her gown."

At the hair salon, Mrs. Campbell continued her insults. She teased Nicole about the texture of her hair and the up-do she chose.

"You've got that back-to-Africa-Goobala-Goobala hair. How many combs do you go through in a week?"

"Hope, I've got to go get my final fitting for the dress. Don't want to be late for dress rehearsal." She winked at Hope, continued, "So I'll meet you at The Falls. Enjoy the rest of your day."

"Nicole, you didn't drive."

"I'll get a cab." She shook her head, whispered, "If that old biddy says one more thing to me, I'm gonna lose it."

In a sing-song voice, Hope said, "Nicole, I need you." She walked to the stylist. "We are a bit pressed for time and need to get ready for rehearsal. How much longer before Mrs. Campbell is ready?"

"Five minutes."

"Thanks. Nicole, give me five minutes, please."

"All right."

Back on the base, the ladies met up with Mica. Hope ran to him.

"Hey honey, I missed you."

"I missed you more."

They kissed until Mica's mother interrupted.

"Hello? Mica, show your mother some love too, dear."

Mica hugged her, kissed her on the cheek.

"You know I love you, Mom. So you guys hung out all day and you're both smiling. I am impressed."

"Don't be silly, son, Hope is delightful. She reminds me of myself at her age. Your taste could not be more astonishing."

"You taught me well, Mom."

"I did indeed."

"Nicole, hey girl. You good?"

"Of course, you know how I do."

"Mom, Nicole is one of the people I owe for keeping us together. Hope was trying to kick me to the curb when Nicole intervened."

"How on earth was Nicole instrumental in your relationship? I am quite certain she lacks the knowledge to accomplish such a task."

"Mom, that was not nice. Apologize to Nicole."

"Let it go, Mica. Your mom has been dogging me all day. I'm starting to enjoy her shrewdness." Nicole looked around Mica. "Speaking of enjoy, who is that fine brotha?"

"That's André. Hope, I forgot to tell you that your boy called while you were at the spa. We swung over and picked him up from the airport."

"Thanks Mica. Ooh I have a good man." She did a full-body shimmy. "Come on, Nicole. I want you to meet my buddy."

~~~~~~~~

The entire party arrived on time and rehearsal ran without a hitch. Hope's anal attention to detail outlined the floor plan, wedding party line up and starting time for every aspect of the ceremony. An hour later, the group caravanned to dinner. Since the wedding coordinator, Hope Tolliver, had made reservations, the hostess escorted the twelve folks to a private room upon arrival. The engaged couple sat across from each other. Occasional glances of affection and the light conversations eased Hope's anxiety, until Vince harassed the waitress.

"Look, sweetie. I know you're probably new at this, but I'm gonna need you to pick up the pace. Got places to go and being late is not an option."

"I apologize, sir. One of the waitresses called in si---"

Vince threw up his hand. "Not trying to hear the sob story, honey bunch. Just get our food out here, pronto!"

Hope glared at Mica, pursed her lips. She didn't want to speak out against his friend, so she expected him to handle the unnecessary rudeness.

"Come on, Vince. That's not cool, man. Give the lady
~~~~~~~~

time to do her job."

"Whatever, dude."

A blonde-haired waitress brought the food to the table about ten minutes later. When she placed Vince's meal in front of him, he reached over to smell her arm.

"Mmm, girl you smell good enough to eat. What's that you're wearing?"

"Spaghetti sauce."

"Oh, you've got jokes. How about you join us for a little fun later tonight?"

"No thank you, sir. Careful, the plate is very hot."

"And so are you." Vince licked his lips, kissed the air.

Hope looked at her civilized guests, shook her head. Her foot tapped under the table. André placed his hand on her knee, gave her a reassuring smile. She sighed as she nibbled at the parmesan chicken.

Vince wolfed down his food. "Mica, hurry it up! The party starts at nine and I've still got to get some singles!" He used the cloth napkin to wipe the red sauce from around his mouth and then belched. "Let's do this."

Hope tensed and began to stand. André grabbed her hand and forced her back to her seat. He widened his eyes, shook his head.

"Excuse me, all. I've got to speak with my fiancé." She jerked away from Dré. "Honey, can I see you for a second?" She flashed a cheesy smile to her guests, nodded her head toward the other end of the room.

Mica continued to eat. Hope walked around the table with a gentle touch on the shoulder of each guest like Duck, Duck, Goose. When she got to the goose, she sat on his lap, whispered in his ear.

"I need to talk to you right now." She stood. With a

stern but playful grip, she led Mica to the lobby. The bewilderment on his face only served to stir up Hope's frustration.

"Mica, I thought we agreed neither of us would have bachelor parties."

"Didn't we have this same conversation yesterday?"

Mica's flippant comment caught Hope off guard. Before she realized it, she had her finger pointed inches from his face.

"I know you don't think I'm going to---"

Dré stepped in between the quarreling couple. "Hey guys I just came to check on you. Is everything okay?"

Mica glared at Dré like a lion vying for his place as king of the pride. "You okay with us getting married?"

"Mica! Dré is just a friend. Why are you acting so childish?"

With his hands lifted in surrender, Dré said, "Hey, I'm not trying to intrude or overstep my boundaries. I just wanted to make sure you guys were okay. I'm going back to the table."

"Wait, Dré. Please excuse Mica's rude remark. His friends seem to be rubbing off on him."

"Yeah, Dré. I apologize. I'm just a little stressed about the wedding."

"You're stressed? What exactly have you done to be stressed?"

Dré tried to thwart off the confrontation. "Hope, don't start---"

"No, Dré. I am sick of---"

Dré put his hand over Hope's mouth and finished her sentence. "She's sick of not being with you and can't wait until tomorrow. Isn't that right, Hope?" With his hand still over her mouth, he spread his fingers so that her agreement could be heard.

Hope refused to answer so Dré removed his hand from her mouth. She crossed her arms in a huff and stared down the men.

Mica shook his head. "Oh, she's throwing a little temper tantrum. Anyway, look I'm sorry about my comment. Why don't you come out with us tonight and we'll make amends?"

"Cool. You guys are leaving at nine, right?"

"Yeah, from the lobby so we'll see you then?"

"Sure, if that's cool with your boys."

"I got this."

Hope put her hand on her hip. "Fine! You go out with your boys. Just remember what you do in the dark will come to light!" She gathered her composure, smiled, returned to the table as if life was perfect.

Chapter Nineteen

Ryan

Everyone returned to the lobby of the base hotel. The girls decided to relax and turn in early. Mica, his boys and Dré left to mingle with women of the night who exchange one-dollar bills for freaky favors. By midnight, the female bridesmaids were asleep. Hope took the quiet time as an opportunity to finalize unfinished personal business.

"Lord, I thank You for being my all sufficiency. I know that it was You who guided me and protected me through my journey to find love. You were there all the time waiting, with open arms, for me to recognize You as my first and last love. Now Lord, let me enter into this covenant with a pure heart. Show me how to love my husband Your way; to be the wife You called me to be; to make Mica my ministry. I'm ready to live my life as a virtuous woman. I want my husband to call me blessed. I want our children to call me blessed. I want to bring honor to Mica and You.

"Before I stand before You and commit my life to Mica, I ask that You break the soul ties I created with David, Tommy, Richard, Ryan and Rafael. Forgive me for stepping out of Your will. I don't want to bring those men into my marriage. Free me from the bondage that has held me hostage. Release Your anointing so that I flow with love, kindness, compassion and respect toward my husband. In Your mighty and matchless name, the name of Jesus, amen."

She picked up the phone and dialed Ryan's number, praying that his wife not be awakened. She took several deep breaths as the phone rang.

"Hello?"

Just above a whisper, Hope said, "Ryan, it's Hope."

"Hey, Hope how have you been?"

"I've been good."

"What's up with cha?"

"I don't know how to ask this, so here it goes…Ryan are you married?"

"Yes as a matter of fact I am, why?"

"André is here for my wedding and he casually brought up attending yours a little over a year ago."

"Oh, so you're getting married?"

"Yes, this Saturday."

"You mean tomorrow?"

"Yeah, I guess it is tomorrow."

"Tell me you are not marrying Tommy."

"No, I haven't talked to him in a minute."

"I was going to say that would have been a ridiculously long engagement."

"Tommy was psychotic to put it mildly."

"I told you that a long time ago but you weren't trying to hear me. So who are you marrying? Anyone I know?"

"No, you don't know him. His name is Mica."

"Oh, now I get it. You are contacting all of your ex-boyfriends to release the news."

"No, why are you trying to turn this around on me? Tell me that you are not still bitter about what happened while you were here."

"No, Hope. I am not bitter but I do resent the way you played me."

"The way I played you? You were up in my face knowing full well that your wife was at home!"

"So that's what this is about?"

"Yes. Were you ever going to tell me?"

"Why are you so upset? What does my marriage have to do with you?"

"Are you kidding me? You tried to sleep—no, impregnate me—while you were married. That doesn't strike you as wrong? Can you say adultery?"

"Don't sound so disturbed. Would it have really made a difference if you'd known I was married?"

"Are you nuts? Of course it would have made a difference, you egotistical, self-centered jerk."

"Wow, Hope. Give me a break. Adultery and fornication are both sins so what's the difference?"

"I believed you when you told me you wanted to be with me forever. What if I'd slept with you and conceived again? You never cared about our baby or me. You don't care about anybody but yourself."

"I guess I deserved that but it's not true. I told you before, you're the one who is loved."

"Then I feel sorry for your wife!"

"Calm down, mama. I'm not as calculating and scandalous as you're making me out to be."

"Did you tell her about us?"

"Didn't have to; she knew I was in love with you when she married me."

"So you knew and she knew yet you didn't bother to enlighten me?"

"I'm a man; a man who wanted to believe you would always be an option. I knew that you'd refuse to be if you found out I was married thus the secrecy."

"For the record, Ryan, you really did a number on me."

"And you're still going to marry that dude tomorrow?"

"What do you think?"

"Of course you are. I married Danielle and I never stopped loving you."

"So is she a teacher or did you lie about that too?"

"Yes, she is and she really does remind me of you."

"Imitation is the ultimate compliment."

"Then tell me about your man. Is he anything like me? Did he put a spell on you? He must be a bad boy because I gave it all I had and still couldn't convince you to marry me."

Hope giggled. "Hilarious. Our thing was bad timing. I had a lot of baggage when we first started dating. I've grown a lot since then." She paused to reminisce about the good times with Ryan.

"You there?" His words snapped her back to present day.

"For instance, remember when you asked me if I was afraid?"

"Yeah, I remember every word I ever said to you."

"Well I was. No one ever got to me the way you did. Followed by the baby situation, I almost lost mind."

"I still can't believe you went through that alone."

"I know but I wasn't really alone, God was there."

"For what it's worth, you would've been a great mom." He chortled like an infant. "You were still my baby's mamma."

"Are you ever going to let that go?"

"Doubtful. It's so amusing because you come off as," he mimicked an English accent, "prim and proper."

"Keep your day job, dude. I'm going to let you go. Don't want the little lady restricting your phone privileges."

Sarcasm invaded his tone, "Ha, ha. You are so funny to me."

"Not bad for a prude."

Ryan snapped his finger as if he remembered something. "There was something I wanted to tell you."

"Oh, Lord. What is it?"

"I can't remember."

"Well it was either a lie or unimportant."

"Whatever. I just hope this guy makes you happy. You deserve to be."

"You amaze me, Ryan. I guess that's why I fell in love with you."

"Me, you're the enigma. You have my number so keep in touch. Remember what we agreed to in college?"

"Can't say that I do."

"To remain friends even if we married other people."

"There's no way! We shot past friendship a long time ago. It's impossible to reverse our feelings."

He sighed. "I know and I never stopped desiring you."

"Me, too. That's why we can't be friends. Gotta end this now before you make me cry."

His tone softened. "Please don't cry. Your eyes puff like Garfield's. Can't have my girl looking crazy on her wedding day."

"You remember the smallest details about me."

"It's called love; you should try it some time."

Hope titled her head up to hold back the flood, but it

didn't work.

"You crying?"

Between gentle sobs, she said, "I love you, Ryan."

"Love you forever. Get at me, Hope."

By the grace of God, another tremendous weight lifted. Hope needed to purge her past before starting a future with Mica. The newfound peace cradled Hope and lulled her into a restful sleep, but before the sun crested the horizon, the phone shrilled.

Lying on her stomach, Hope's hand searched the nightstand for the phone. "Hel---" She dropped it, retrieved it, "Hello?"

"I was wrong."

"Dré?" She lifted her head off the pillow to look at the clock. It took a moment for her eyes to focus. She yawned, rested the phone on her face, talked into the pillow. "You okay?"

"Yeah, yeah, wake up!"

"What's wrong with you?"

"It's not me; it's your boy. He's drunk out of his mind."

Her eyes widened. She grabbed the phone, rolled over, sat up in bed. "Mica doesn't drink anymore. Where are you?"

"Some club downtown. I can't recall the name."

"Is it a strip club?"

"No, but it might as well be. These girls are half-naked and they are all over your man."

"Dré, shut up!"

"I'm serious. I've been looking out for you and up until now he's been behaving. But I'm telling you, things are about to go all wrong. His boys have a hotel room and they're planning to take these girls there after we leave the club. One freak has been flirting with Mica all night. He blew her off earlier, but now that he's downed a few drinks, I'm convinced his judgment is beyond impaired. You need to get to the hotel and fast."

"Dré, do you really think I should come down? If he'd throw away our relationship on a one-night stand, he's probably not the one for me. Maybe I should just let the night play itself out and see what happens."

"Time out for game playing. I think he's a keeper, he's just made some poor decisions tonight. Not that he's done anything out of the way… at least not yet. I just don't want him to blow it. You deserve to be happy and he makes you smile with a glow I've never seen before."

"But---"

"I don't have time to baby you through one of your fits. Get to the hotel ASAP!"

"Should I wake up Nicole?"

"Why would you do that?"

"Moral support."

"That's what I'm here for."

"Quick, what's the name of the hotel?"

"You got pen and paper? Vince is loading up the car with girls as we speak."

Hope scribbled the address, threw on a jogging suit, sped to the hotel. As she pulled into the parking lot, she spotted Dré waving her over to a side-entry door.

"Come on, girl. They've been in the room for twenty minutes."

Hope slammed the car door, ran up the sidewalk. "Long enough to get busy."

Dré opened the door. "Don't think like that."

They raced up the stairs skipping every other step.

Hope asked, "How are we going to get into the room?"

"I told them that I had to light up the toilet and was going to use the one in the lobby. They're keeping the door propped open for me."

"That is so nasty. A free-for-all opened to the general pubic."

"Public?"

"I said what I meant."

At the third floor, Hope gestured for Dré to be quiet. They tiptoe-sprinted down the hall to room 316.

Outside the door, Hope whispered, "For Mica so loved the whore…"

Dré tightened his lips and mouthed Stop it. He pushed the door open, walked in first. The well-lit room looked like a brothel. Vince was on the floor in mid-stroke. Chris was entangled with a female on the over-sized chair. Mike, Jason and three hussies occupied the queen-sized bed closest to the door. Flashes of flesh made Hope take a step back. She threw her hand over her mouth to capture the gasp fighting to get out.

Hope's gawking rested on Mica and the whore lying with him on the other bed. He was stripped to his boxers, she wore a black Victoria Secret thong and matching lace bra. Hope stepped around Vince, kicked him as she walked past. He never broke rhythm.

"Mica Campbell, what are you doing?" She grabbed a pillow off the floor and smacked Mica with it. With a slight pause after each word, she said, "Get up and get dressed!"

Vicki Secret took a dive under the cover.

Hope snatched the lining off the bed and glared at her.

"Excuse me, whore, is there a problem?"

She kept her eyes on Hope, used her right hand to search for her clothes. "Who are you?"

"Don't act like you haven't seen me around the dorms. I don't know your name, but I know you're desperate and pathetic." She looked over to Mica to make sure he was getting dressed, back to the whore. "Only way for you to get a man is to prey on one who's drunk and happily engaged, huh?" Hope threw a pink mini-skirt at her.

"If he's so happily engaged, what is he doing here with me?"

Hope leaned forward, squared her shoulders, made herself bigger. "Somebody must have prayed for you." She pulled the gun from her leg holster, put it in the trollop's face. "I left the bullets at home."

Vicki squealed, wet the bed.

Hope cocked one eyebrow, turned up her nose. "Clean yourself up and get out of here."

Mica stood with his shirt on backwards, his pants at his knees. "Hope, honey is that you?"

She bit her lip to halt the profanity, but venom spewed out nonetheless. "Yes, stupid, I'm here. Pass out or something already."

Vicki dipped into the bathroom, while the rest of the Campbell crew got back to business. Mica zipped his pants and followed Hope and Dré to the car.

From the backseat, Mica slurred, "Hope, lis...listen to me. It's not what it looks like." He fanned off imaginary canaries circling his head. "Let's go back to the room so I can expl---"

Hope sat in the passenger seat, crossed her arms. "I don't think so, loser! Judging by your actions we should call off the wedding. You're not ready for true covenant."

"You-you know I love you. If you leave me I-I-I…" He drifted to sleep, then awoke. "I'd go crazy!"

"Too late!"

"Don't do this to me."

"Shut up, stupid. I warned you, but you refused to listen."

"I know and I'm sorry," he whined. "So are you going to leave me for André? Please, please don't leave me or," he slapped his hands on the seat, "I'll cry."

"Who cares if you cry? I don't even know why I'm trying to rationalize with your drunk behind. Just pass out."

Dré looked at Mica through the rearview mirror then turned toward Hope. "Are you really thinking about calling off the wedding?"

"Yes I am and rightfully so. If you hadn't gone with them, do you think his friends would have called me? Who knows what would have happened had we not intervened."

"To add insult to injury, his boys think you and I are messing around."

"What? Why would they assume that?"

"I have no idea. All I know is Vince kept questioning our friendship; implying that we were sexually involved. He instigated the entire night."

"I'm not surprised. He really bugs me."

A voice echoed from the backseat. "Hey, you two I'm still awake."

"Shut up, Mica. Who cares?"

"That comment was so unnecessary. Why are you treating Mica like he's a child?"

"Because he's acting like one. You should know, you babysat him tonight. What man requires a babysitter?"

"None, but you said he was the one."

"Dré?"

"Yeah."

"You can shut up, too."

Dré furrowed his brows, added bass to his voice, annunciated each word. "I'm a grown man and I will not tolerate your indignant behavior." He relaxed his countenance, returned to his normal pattern of speech. "I just want to see you happy. Don't make a hasty decision based on one night."

"Why would you say that?"

"You are notorious for making them."

"So what, who asked you? Wait; before you shut up..." She looked back at Mica, shook her head, continued, "You're my best friend in the whole wide world. I appreciate your endurance, especially for tolerating all of my drama."

"Not a problem. I love you."

"Give me hug."

"Do you not see this steering wheel in my hands?"

"Don't care, give me hugs."

Dré patted Hope on the back with his right hand, controlled the car with his left. "Where do you want to stay tonight? You still trying to sleep in separate rooms?"

"As much as I'd love to hang out in your room, it would look bad. I better stay with Mica."

"Good try but that's not what I meant. I thought you didn't want Mica to see you."

"I didn't but so much for that. I don't want anyone, especially his mom, to know about tonight so that means

I've got to nurse him back to health."

"I would do it but I don't know him like that."

"Appreciate you, but that's my job. I'll do it but he owes me… big time!"

Even before taking the vow to love, honor and cherish, Hope endured the "in sickness" part. She stayed up all night with her husband-to-be. Mica moaned, groaned and vomited every few minutes. After the fourth failed attempt to get him into the bathroom before the expulsion, she helped him into the tub. Whatever excretions hit the floor, she wiped clean. All other bodily fluids got rinsed down the drain. As Mica drifted in and out of sleep, he told Hope that he loved her each time he opened his eyes. She made a pallet on the floor to garner some beauty sleep between episodes.

Somewhere in the state between REM sleep and semi-consciousness, Hope replayed the events leading up to the night's fiasco. Strike one: The day they went to obtain the marriage license, Hope stepped into a pond of knee-deep mud. The brown sludge spotted her white mini skirt, soiled her matching tennis shoes. Strike two: Hope fainted in the courthouse lobby. Mica caught her just before her limp body hit the floor. Strike three: The bachelor bash. She couldn't explain her compulsion to follow through with the wedding.

The next day, Hope woke up in the bed. Mica stood over her with a tray in his hands.

"Mica, what have you done?" Still under the covers, she sat up.

"I promise I will never drink again. I know it doesn't make up for last night but," he placed the tray across her lap, fluffed the pillow supporting her back. "I brought you twelve long-stemmed roses and your favorite: pancakes smothered in strawberries."

"Nice try." She inhaled the fresh-off-the-griddle pancakes. "Where did you find jade roses?"

"They're not really jade; I dyed white roses." He sparkled a full grin, poured maple syrup on her food. "But hey, I love you." He raised his eyebrows. "We okay? You forgive me?"

"We are not okay, Mica. I stayed up all night cleaning up your vomit when I should have been sleeping like a princess in preparation for my special day." She cut into the pancakes, stabbed a forkful, stuffed her mouth. "I forgive you. Not because I want to but because God says so."

"You still want to marry me?"

She used the linen napkin to wipe the excess syrup from her mouth. "Of course, mighty man of God, I love you." She kissed the air, shoveled in more food. "Let's put this behind us and get to the happily ever after."

"I love you so much!"

They kissed.

Hope mugged his head. "You better. Come on, we need to get going. What time is it?"

"Two."

"Two as in p.m.?" She moved the tray, threw her legs to the side of the bed. "The wedding starts in two hours! Get out of my way so I can get into the shower. Come on Mica, chop chop." She ran into the bathroom.

Mica stood in the doorway. "Hope, do you really love me?"

"Yes, is there a reason I shouldn't?"

"No. How much do you love me?"

"I love you a whole hugga hugga bunch."

"For how long?"

"Always and forever."

"Good. You know you really are the only one for me. I want to change our wedding song to *Only One for Me* by Brian McKnight."

"I don't think so."

"What's wrong with it?"

"Well for starters it's one-sided. I mean he's telling the woman that he'll be the man she needs him to be like he messed up and wants to make things right."

"Doesn't that seem fitting?"

"Who wants a wedding song that reminds them of their mate's recklessness?"

"It doesn't. It professes his undying love for her."

"Well what about her love for him?"

"He doesn't care as long as he treats her right for the rest of their lives."

"Hmm, I kind of like that. Okay we'll change it. Call the DJ and make sure he has that CD."

"I'm sure he does."

"Call him anyway, Mica. I'm getting in the shower."

Chapter Twenty

Mica

The afternoon sun splashed rays of light through the dense foliage that surrounded The Falls. The flowers in full bloom arrayed the landscape like a rainbow and sprinkled a delicate scent into the air. The sound of a flowing stream and chirping birds soothed the heart.

A waterfall cascaded a few feet behind the officiating minister. He stood at the center of the small island with the wedding party on either side of him. A bridge connected the island to the mainland shore where the guests were seated in white, wooden chairs.

Hope wore a non-traditional knee-length gown. With a sleeveless bodice and a removable train embellished with lavish beading, the gown transformed into a party dress in less than a minute; perfect for island dancing. Her bouquet was made of white and lilac flowers indigenous to the area.

As she strolled across the bridge, Hope gazed at her man. Instead of a tuxedo, Mica chose to wear his dress blues, the Air Force's equivalent to black-tie formal wear. The dark blue jacket had antiqued silver buttons and colorful miniature medals on the left chest. He wore matching blue trousers, bow tie, cummerbund. The shoulder boards exaggerated his girth and the silver wrist braids identified him as an officer. His full smile framed the look.

Anxious to start her life with Mica, Hope's knees shook. She wobbled in the three-inch sandals and teetered on the narrow strip of island. Dré flinched each time she wobbled. On the third stagger, he pulled her to the side. They stood near the waterfall to drown out the conversation.

"Hope, are you okay?"

She fanned herself with the bouquet. "I'm okay. Just a little nervous."

"I need you to quit all that rocking. It feels like an earthquake on this little island and I'm afraid you're going to fall into the water."

"I'm fine. I just can't seem to stand still."

"Maybe this is another sign that you shouldn't do this."

"But last night you told me to do it."

"Only because I thought it was what you wanted. Is it?"

"Yes..." Hope wobbled and Dré reached to stable her. "Unless you can give me a reason why I shouldn't."

"That's not my call, Hope. I just want you to be h---"

"Happy, I know. I'd be happier if he hadn't had that ridiculous bachelor party."

"You said that no one could rain on your parade. If you've forgiven him, why are you bringing it up?"

"Am I supposed to be over it?"

"Yeah, if you're going to marry him. You can't hold it over his head."

Hope adjusted her train. "Do you think I should marry him or not?"

"That is not my decision. Take a deep breath and join

us at the altar or run. Either way I got your back." He swooped Hope's bangs back in place. "Decide and do it quickly."

Still fanning with the bouquet, she looked into the waterfall. The serenity of the natural formation soothed her into a momentary trance. As the gentle mist danced around her, Hope chose to commit to her Father and her husband. No turning back, no giving up. She reflected on the words of Pastor Berger, *Come back to your first love*, yielded her will to the Lord's. From this day forward, whatever was required of her as wife and chosen vessel, she would honor.

She looked at Dré, extended her hand to him, said, "I'm ready."

He took her hand, kissed her forehead, escorted her to her position next to Mica.

Mica nodded at Dré, took Hope's hand, turned to the minister.

The ceremony continued as did Hope's wobbling. Other than her family not being in attendance, the remainder of the day was perfect. The newlyweds slipped away as Nicole and Dré took care of any unfinished ceremonial business.

Since their flight for Nassau didn't leave until the next day, they checked into Embassy Suites. Mica carried Hope into the room. Jasmine-scented candles and jade-colored rose petals made a path to the bed. Toni Braxton's *I Love Me Some Him* caressed the room.

Mica laid Hope on the bed, restated his undying love for her. She quivered in his arms, whispered her commitment to him. The Campbells marked the beginning of their happily ever after.

Approval

All my life I have longed for,
yearned for, searched for,
Approval
Approval from my friends
and... the step who married my mother
But stairs were never sufficient enough
to walk, run, cry, or lie on level ground
Deceitful towards everyone
Struggling to fit in
Fantasy became reality
Exaggeration my second skin
it shielded and protected acts,
I knew were sins
Tormented from within. Would it ever end?
Mother had a family so tightly weaved and blessed
her children were wounded, cursed, with only pain
to confess
But then I found God
an unconditional love, an eternal love
Consumed, I lost the old me... and found approval

About Joy Marino

Joy Marino has traveled across America as a "military brat." Interacting with a diversity of people during her childhood, she became fluent in Spanish.

She obtained a bachelor's degree in psychology and minored in dance at the University of Cincinnati. Joy is a veteran of the United States Air Force. Her military career began with intelligence operations and concluded with database management. After serving her country for four years, she returned to Cincinnati as a professional educator. She teaches high school Spanish.

Joy enjoys motivational speaking, dancing and writing poetry and novels. Her first published work is *The Joy of the Lord is My Strength* in *Tainted Mirror An Anthology* published by Pen of the Writer. The true story portrays Joy's struggle with depression after a series of life-changing events including a miscarriage, a critically ill child and diagnosis of breast cancer. She expounds on her pilgrimage to healing and eventual victory over depression.

Joy resides in Ohio with her wonderful husband and two beautiful daughters.

MySpace.com/JoyMarino

About Valerie Coleman

Valerie L. Coleman has been called to help writers get their books published. Walking in her purpose, she established **Pen Of the WritER** or POWER. She has coached hundreds of aspiring authors through the process of writing and publishing. With a heart to teach and serve, she founded the **Pen to Paper Literary Symposium** in 2004. Past presenters include national best-selling authors Dan Poynter, Lynnette Khalfani, Vickie Stringer and Kendra Norman-Bellamy.

Eager to invest in joint collaborations, Valerie is a founding member of **Soul of the Pen**. The objective of this cadre of Christian authors is to use the written word to develop healthy relationships and strengthen families. Partnering with Dr. Vivi Monroe Congress, she formed **Queen V Publishing** to transform manuscripts into polished works of art.

Valerie has transitioned into the arts & entertainment industry. Through her talent agency, **Prose Rhythm and Praise**, she provides clean entertainment: music artists, authors, comedians, dancers and producers. She manages several artists including the gospel trio, **Christopher**.

Valerie has a bachelor's degree in industrial engineering from GMI Engineering & Management Institute and an MBA from the University of Dayton. She is a college mathematics instructor. She resides in Dayton, Ohio, with her husband, Craig. They worship at Revival Center Ministries, International.

PenoftheWriter.com   QueenVPublishing.net

Paul Mitchell Ministries

The sermon in Chapter Five is an excerpt from the message *I Need a King; Give Me a King* by Pastor Paul Mitchell (April 17, 2005).

Pastor Paul, a moniker given to him by the youth he pastors, has appeared on Trinity Broadcast Network (TBN) and The Word Network. He has ministered with international speakers Bishop Eddie Long, Bishop Andrew Merritt and Dr. Mark Hanby.

Committed to having a positive impact on the community, Pastor Paul sponsors book bag giveaways, clothing giveaways and food drives. He serves as vice chairman of Project Impact-Dayton; a not-for-profit agency organized and operated to provide comprehensive prevention, intervention and educational services to Montgomery-County youth and their families.

Pastor Paul has international vision. He has traveled to Egypt, Israel and Jerusalem providing medical care, food and encouragement to citizens who reside in garbage dumps and isolated villages.

Combining wisdom, biblical principles and sprinkles of humor, Pastor Paul provides solutions for today's problems to more than 1000 congregants as senior pastor of Revival Center Ministries, International.

PaulMitchellMinistries.org
PO Box 60362
Dayton, Ohio 45406
937.307.0760
PaulMitchellMin@aol.com

OCIR Business

The presentation about abortion in Chapter Eleven was created by Ashton L. Wilson.

Ashton L. Wilson is a writer, speaker and ambassador of Christ. A passionate man of influence, he was called to spread the Kingdom gospel and help others.

Wilson owns and operates OCIR Business—a Cincinnati-based, non-profit organization and design consulting firm. The intent of OCIR is to provide the under-facilitated community with quality design and small business consulting services including

- Website design and hosting
- graphic design and printing
- business-plan development
- advertising and marketing strategy
- image consultation
- philanthropy

OCIR Business - A company built on faith!
901 Elm Street
Cincinnati, Ohio 45202
877.357.OCIR (6247)
info@ocirbusiness.com
OCIRBusiness.com

"Making your vision become real, one step at a time"

Queen V Publishing
The Doorway to YOUR Destiny!

Go thou and publish abroad the kingdom of God.
—Luke 9:60

We are a Christian contract publisher committed to transforming manuscripts into polished works of art. **Queen V Publishing** —a company of standard and integrity — offers an alternative that allows God's word in YOU to do what it was sent to do for OTHERS. Submit your manuscript online or by postal mail. Visit the website for complete guidelines and the contract plan that best fits your literary goals and needs.

QueenVPublishing.net

We help experts master self-publishing!

Valerie L. Coleman
Queen V Publishing
Dayton, Ohio
937.307.0760
Info@PenoftheWriter.com

Pen of the Writer

*Out of Ephraim was there a root of them against Amalek; after thee, Benjamin, among thy people; out of Machir came down governors, and out of Zebulun they that handle the **pen of the writer**.*
~ Judges 5:14

Pen **Of** the Writ**ER**

A Christian publishing company committed to using the writing pen as a weapon to fight the enemy and celebrate the good news of Christ Jesus.

Taking writers from pen to paper to published!

Passionate Pens
Write On! Workshop
Pen to Paper Literary Symposium
Literary Management & Consultation

Pen of the Writer, LLC
Dayton, Ohio
937.307.0760
PenoftheWriter.com
info@PenoftheWriter.com

Prose, Rhythm and Praise

Your resource for clean entertainment

Prose, Rhythm and Praise provides management, promotions and booking for music artists, comedians, actors and more!

The *Prose, Rhythm and Praise* Internet talk show, hosted by Valerie Coleman, airs the first Thursday of every month at 9:00 pm EST.

Enjoy chats with national recording artists, best-selling authors and other experts in the Arts & Entertainment industry. Listen and participate during the live show at BlogTalkRadio.com/ChurchOhio.

To book clean entertainment for your event, contact us at Info@PenoftheWriter.com or 937.307.0760

ProseRhythmAndPraise.com

Lord, Help Me to Hold Out

Order additional copies of

Lord, Help Me to Hold Out

Joy Marino
PO Box 364
West Chester, Ohio 45071
QueenVPublishing.net
JoyMarino71@yahoo.com

* * * * * * * * * * * * * * * * *

Please mail ______ copies of

Lord, Help Me to Hold Out

____
Name

____
Address

____
City / State / Zip
(______)________________________________
Phone

____
Email

Quantity	Price Per Book	Total
	$14.95	
Sales Tax (OH residents add $1.05 per book)		
Shipping ($2.99 first book, $0.99 each additional)		
Grand Total* (Payable to: Joy Marino)		

* Certified check and money orders only